Weekend Wedding DECEPTION

(A Dangerous Millionaire Novel)

Debra Andrews

ELUSIVE STAR PRESS

ISBN: 978-0-9881805-5-0

Editor, Patricia Thomas

Photos for cover from:
bigstockphoto.com
RomanceNovelCovers.com

Printed in the U.S.A.

DEDICATION

This book is dedicated to my husband, daughter, and son. You rock my world.

ACKNOWLEDGMENTS

I'd like to thank all those who helped me with this story: my incredibly patient sisters, critique partners, and my fabulous editor Patricia Thomas.

OTHER BOOKS AVAILABLE BY DEBRA ANDREWS IN THE DANGEROUS MILLIONAIRES SERIES:

(Books can be read in any order and are stand-alone stories)

WEEKEND WEDDING DECEPTION
DANGEROUS PARADISE
DISGUISED WITH THE MILLIONAIRE
HIS WYOMING LAIR (coming 2016)

Sign up for a new releases email, so you can find out when the next book is available:

http://www.debraandrewsauthor.com

CHAPTER ONE

"I hope nothing bad happens this weekend," Carly McAlister said wistfully.

Abby Warren sheared off a long-stemmed red rose and stuffed it into a silver vase. Dressed in a dreamy violet dress, she felt right at home among the flowers. She peered over the roses at her best friend and smiled warmly. "You know every bride is concerned about their upcoming wedding day. You're no exception, but nothing will go wrong."

The two women stood at the marble island in the kitchen of the McAlister family mansion outside the small town of Brookstone.

"Well, Abby, I can tell you that you never know what will happen at a Farrington-McAlister-Drake-Knight event. All those family surnames seem to draw trouble."

The surnames represented a bunch of nephews taken under the wing of Mr. James Farrington, the rich and self-appointed patriarch of the family. They were distant cousins of his grandson Trent. Mr. James Farrington owned the family's ancestral estate when he bought and saved the house from being bulldozed by a developer several years before.

The scent of roses permeated the room, along with delicious smells of food prepared by staff. Many of the guests would arrive that day—Wednesday. Then the formal party that evening would kick off the festivities leading up to the Saturday wedding.

"You're so lucky to have your wedding here. Most women would die for such lavish parties," Abby said as she snipped another red rose.

Dressed in a similar outfit to Abby's, but in chartreuse, Carly nodded. "Uncle James always wanted a big family, and it is kind of him to throw these parties before my wedding. He said he wouldn't dream of letting my mom pay for any costs associated with the wedding either. Well, now, what about you? Tell me, Abby—*who* is he?"

"Who is *who*?" Abby rolled her eyes, knowing she sounded like an owl. She'd expected these questions, as she hadn't seen Carly in over a month.

"It's been two years since Jack. There must be someone," Carly pressed.

Abby drummed her fingers on the cool white-marble counter and avoided eye contact with her friend. "No. No one..."

"Abby, you're talking to *me*."

"All right," Abby said, heat rising on her cheeks. "There is no one new, but Sam Preston asked me out. I went out with him—*as a friend.* He wants to be more, but I don't know. There's something about him that I can't warm up to…"

"What don't you like about him? He's nice looking and he's liked you since high school. He was always trailing after you."

"But we've always been just *friends…*"

"So, you're saying he doesn't give you that special feeling?"

Abby's shoulders drooped and she shook her head. "None at all. And I can't force myself to have feelings if I don't. I'm not sure I'll go out with him again. It's a waste of time for him—and for me." Abby gave her friend a lopsided grin and added, "Dear Carly, not everyone will get what you have with Miles—a glorious love. You two are going to have the happiest marriage, and *I*, for one, am happy for you."

"You're only twenty-six and you act like it will never happen for you. Besides, you've been in love before, Abby. It will happen again."

Abby turned back to the cut flowers and stuffed the long stems into a vase. "False love, Carly. He just wanted me in bed. Jack preferred my roommate for the long haul."

Abby didn't want to turn this into a question and answer session about her life, which had been shades of gray for the past two years since Jack McAlister, the love of her life, ditched her. Not long after he broke up with her, she learned he was dating her ex-roommate. However, even worse, Jack was Carly's cousin, which meant she was likely to run into him when she spent time with Carly.

"I'm just glad Jack won't be here, since, as you said, he's out of the country, right?" Abby asked.

Carly cleared her throat. "Yeah. I did say that. You know, Jack's been in the Middle East doing contract work for over five months. He and Monica—"

"Jack's still with her?" Abby tried to keep that pain from overwhelming her. "That's all I wanted to hear. Let's not talk about them—ever—*please*. I'm just glad he's on the other side of the world."

When Carly's forehead wrinkled, Abby frowned. The gesture reminded her so much of Jack. Carly had the same black hair and had also inherited the same vivid green eyes. That reminder caused Abby's heart to ache with loss all over again.

"I just don't know what happened with you two," Carly blurted. "Seeing each other since high school, then in college…afterward. I thought you two were destined to be together forever, like one of those great romances in the movies."

"Jack didn't believe in *our* fairytale. Did you know, he never once told me that he loved me—he said everything else, except those words. He probably thought I was a pain in the neck, and he didn't feel the way I did. Maybe that's why we broke up so many times."

Abby and Jack had met in high school when she was a freshman and he was a senior. Even though sparks had flown between them that year, she had been too young for him. He told her that what she felt was 'puppy love' and teased her about staring at him with her 'flashing blue' eyes. Still, he'd spent time talking with her at school events. She had never hidden her interest, and when he dated older girls, she tried her hardest to hide her hurt.

Then Jack had gone off to college. Abby caught up with him at Ohio State in her freshman year. He was ready to graduate when she began, but this time things changed between them. During that first year, Jack had seen her as the woman she had become and they'd dated. Their first time together had been the start of a hot and heavy romance.

Jack had been her first lover and the love of her life. However, at the end of the year, once again, they separated. He moved on to graduate school in California, while she continued college in Ohio. Her heart had been broken with the loss.

After graduation, when she had a job and an apartment, they saw each other again and picked up where they'd left off and their romance continued for a blissful two years.

Nothing could separate her and Jack again—or so she thought—until Monica Stevens became her roommate. Then Monica began hinting that Jack wasn't as devoted as he seemed.

Even so, during that time, when they were together everything seemed fine. Then Abby got a leave of absence and left for Europe with her family for a three-month vacation. While she was there, she had to call Jack with news that she was sure he'd take badly—

"I'm sorry, too, that you two broke up," Carly said, startling Abby and bringing her back to the present. "We could have been real cousins if you married Jack. And I'm so sorry you were hurt by him."

Abby flicked her friend a wan smile. "I don't hold that against you, Carly," Abby said, teasing, "but after I wrecked his brand new car and drove it into that creek, with his laptop in the trunk... Well I'm sure that didn't help his feelings for me. And you know Jack and I always had an on-again, off-again relationship anyway. Besides, he never wanted children, and I did."

"You know that's probably because Jack raised his brothers when his mother wasn't around. He was jaded about all the responsibility involved with kids. That was hard for him, but I'm sure he will eventually want his own family."

Abby shook her head. "I don't think so, and that makes him perfect, for the *perfect* Monica. She never liked kids. Wouldn't want her body changed by a pregnancy or her lifestyle curbed by raising children. No. If I never—*ever*—see Jack again, that will be too soon for me. And if I do see him, I can assure you I'm over him, and it would be no big deal after all this time."

"Are you sure, Abby? That it would be no big deal?"

Abby threw a sideways glance at her friend. "At one time, Jack was my knight in shining armor, but that knight sure got tarnished when he took a tumble off his horse. I learned he's not to be trusted. In my mind, Jack is all but forgotten. I'm doing fine without him...*really.*" It was all a lie, and she knew it. "Here, let me finish the next vase. I know you have things to do."

"Yeah, I have to double check the menu. I want everything to be perfect. The staff here is making the cake."

"Okay, just give me something I can do to help after I finish this vase."

"Just place these four vases where you think they'll look good in the living areas. Take this one, then come back for the others. We have a few more to fill and then we're done." Carly gave Abby a cheesy grin. "These roses are my favorite color. And with your light hair, you should look smashing in the red gown."

Abby chuckled. "Yeah—*blood* red."

"It's more scarlet, like the roses. When you go out there, please keep your hands tightly on the vase—"

"Because I'm a klutz?"

"No—well maybe a little—but once you step through that door, you'll see what I mean, so have a good grip on those. You have never seen the amount and quality of *eye candy* my cousins present when they're all in one room. And tonight everyone is dressed to kill in formal wear. Most of my cousins are already here."

"I've met a few of them over the years." Including the *cad*, Carly's cousin Jack, Abby thought bitterly.

"Well, I would set you up with one of them, but, honey, I don't want you to get hurt. They're all heartbreakers, so stay away. I will be surprised if any of them get married—except Alex, who already has. However, he's so miserable. He's certainly warned the rest of my cousins off marriage."

Abby chuckled. "Then you're saying look, but don't touch…"

"Exactly. They're all confirmed bachelors and playboys. All lethal to women's hearts."

"You can be sure I'll heed your warning. I've already been burned by one of your handsome cousins, remember?"

"Yeah, Abby, and I don't want you hurt again. But I can't figure out what happened with you two, but I could have sworn Jack really loved you."

Abby held up a stopping hand. "No! Jack must have been into me for only one thing. He liked that well enough. At least until he met my roommate—you know, the *beautiful and perfectly pulled together Monica.* She was just too tempting for him. And I didn't seem to matter after that."

"Are you kidding me? You're much prettier than she is, and from what I hear, she's had a ton of help in the looks department, so much so that Monica is bordering on plastic. She has to work hard to maintain her expensive coordinated designer outfits and beauty routines, too."

Abby raised her chin. "Carly, you're just saying that because you're my friend."

"No, I'm not."

Abby shrugged. "Well, it doesn't matter who Jack sees. He was the one who broke up with me. He always said he was a realist and didn't believe in fairytale romance—and now neither do I." Abby winced at the pained expression on her friend's face, yet restated, "*I don't.*"

"I'm sorry for you then—not the fairytale part—but for how you feel about *love.*"

"Don't worry about me, okay? I'm just glad you're happy. Perhaps I should go out with Sam on a real date…" *Was there something wrong with her?* Jack had moved on two years ago. It was time for her to do the same now that she'd lowered her expectations.

"Abby, just don't settle. Okay? You *loved* Jack."

"Maybe one day I'll believe in the fairytale again—or not. Maybe I'll never get married." With that, Abby headed for the door with the flowers.

Carly called out, "Be careful with the roses—"

"I will, but don't worry so much. The only one who turns me into a klutz is Jack. And, thankfully, he's not here."

Abby stepped into the living room filled with soft jazz music.

Her gaze immediately found Carly's handsome cousins gathered around a table, sitting or standing.

Wow, Carly wasn't kidding. They were all drop-dead gorgeous.

Some of them, Abby had met before. They were all the more striking in their crisp white shirts, black jackets and bow ties.

Then the group shifted and one man came into view.

Abby's heart skipped a beat.

Jack! No. It can't be.

She halted. Tall, and strikingly handsome with hair darker than any midnight sky, there was no doubt Jack stood across the room. Her throat constricted.

Then a woman stepped beside him. *Monica!* Abby's ex-roommate.

Too much blood rushed to Abby's head and the silver vases tumbled to the ground with a loud crash. All eyes turned to her. She pivoted and fled back into the kitchen.

Abby clutched Carly's arm. "J-J-Jack…"

"Oh, no. He's here already?" Carly squeaked.

Abby reared back, her eyes filling with tears. "You knew. Why didn't you warn me?"

"I was trying to break it to you…that a few days ago he changed his plans and said he'd be here for the wedding, but I didn't know he'd arrive four days before the wedding."

Trembling all over, Abby hugged herself and tried to catch her breath. "I'll go home. I-I'll come back right before the wedding. I promise I'll be here for you on Saturday, Carly."

"Please, don't leave. I want you to be here with me for all the fun activities, too."

Abby was torn. "I don't know, Carly…" If she left now she would miss everything they'd planned for the long weekend. And thinking about her reaction to Jack, she'd probably only reacted so strongly because she'd been surprised. These past two years, she had learned to control her feelings, to be numb to the hurt he'd caused. Could she tolerate being in the same room with him at functions over the next few days for the sake of her best friend? Could she? She had been devastated by him, but it was time to grow up.

"He doesn't know you're my Maid of Honor," Carly confided. "When Miles's brother David broke his leg, Jack's plans had changed, and he was available again. You know we originally wanted Jack in the wedding party. He was unavailable with those contracts he had to fulfill in the Middle East. And he and Miles are such good friends…"

Abby's shoulders drooped. "You mean Jack's the Best Man? That's even worse, Carly! I'll have to stand up with him at the ceremony and participate in some activities with him."

As she considered that, the pain of her loss and of how much she had loved him hit like a rogue wave again. Tears slid down her cheeks.

Carly handed Abby a paper towel. "Oh, I'm so sorry. I was afraid to tell you. Thought you might bail on us, but you're not a coward, Abby, are you? I need and want your support and I'll make it up to you. Promise."

At the look on her friend's face, Abby sucked in a deep breath to settle her nerves. "No, I'm not a coward…but I admit that seeing Jack is a stunner."

Carly seemed to relax on an exhale, as if she knew Abby wouldn't desert her. "You'll stay, won't you?"

Abby blotted her eyes and nodded. Then she smiled through her tears. "Do you think I can avoid him the entire weekend? Hide behind the houseplants perhaps, duck below tables of food?" she quipped lightly, trying to ease her friend's concerns.

"You'll probably knock them over."

"I'm sorry I dropped the flowers."

"Don't worry. Martha will clean up the damage, but I am worried about you."

Resolving that she would bolster her courage and her pride and get through this debacle, she straightened her shoulders. "We're all adults here. We're not in high school. If he can move on, so can I, Carly. I don't know why I haven't already."

And really, why hadn't she? The big question was how would she get through this long, *long*, week of parties and the wedding on Saturday with Jack in the same house?

CHAPTER TWO

An hour earlier, Jack McAlister had arrived at the white brick mansion with his girlfriend, Monica, intending to be part of the week's celebrations and then the wedding party on the weekend. They climbed the steps to the front porch that overlooked a sweeping lawn and a sparkling lake. A valet had driven off to park Jack's rental car.

After he and Monica settled their suitcases in their room, they proceeded downstairs. Monica saw this week as a way to be accepted into his large family, but Jack wasn't so sure he wanted that. He feigned a smile to make Monica happy, but was uncomfortable as he felt the noose tightening...

Monica's eyes sparkled with anticipation as they entered the room. At least fifty people were gathered off the foyer.

Jack crossed the floor to meet his cousins who stood at a large round mahogany table. All but a few had already arrived and were chatting together. They were a tall lot, like Jack, and sometimes could be rowdy—but they were also decent guys. A common ancestor, a long-deceased great-great-great-great grandmother and grandfather, William and Rebecca McAlister, related them all. As pioneers, that couple had traveled from the east coast to Ohio by wagon and on horseback, along with their young sons in the early 1800s.

Although Jack and his cousins now lived all over the globe, Trent's grandfather, James Farrington, kept them bonded together as a family as a tribute to his late wife, Eliza McAlister Farrington. While James Farrington had no blood relationship to Jack's distant cousins, his love for his 'dear Eliza' and his goodwill had shaped them all into a family.

Jack had been about to say hello to his cousins when he turned his head and saw a vase of red roses crash to the floor. A woman—an angelic vision with long, sun-streaked blond hair—whirled away before his eyes.

And a sledgehammer hit Jack's heart.

Abby? It couldn't be.

He stared at the woman who hurried away to the kitchen in a violet blur.

Neither Carly, nor Miles, had mentioned that Abby would be here. They knew he never wanted to see her again—they would have warned him.

Jack took in a deep breath to recover. Like he had so many times in the past two years.

He hadn't seen the woman's face from the front, but perhaps it was only a resemblance to Abby... That had to be it—she was just another beautiful woman who resembled his ex.

His shoulders sagged in relief. He thought he'd put Abby and the past behind him, and he'd be happy never to see her again.

It was only natural, wasn't it? That now, when he was back in Ohio, his memories of Abby would be stirred to the surface—that he would see her in other women who bore any kind of resemblance. He should have come alone so he could focus, but Monica had begged him to take this next big step, and introduce her to his large family. And he knew she would expect a ring to follow. The thought of being engaged to Monica agitated and depressed him.

At thirty-one years old, however, it was time to make *his* plans for his future, and it wasn't fair to string Monica along and remain in a relationship if it wasn't going to go anywhere. During the first three months he was away in the Middle East, he thought—rather, he hoped—that she would grow impatient with him and break if off, but she'd called and said the opposite: When he came back she wanted to make their relationship official. That's when he extended his contract for two months, hoping she'd grow tired of waiting and she'd go out and meet someone else. She hadn't.

Now, he was back, and it was time to make decisions.

Needing some support after the reminder of Abby, he took a detour to the bar and ordered a Scotch on the rocks. Jack took a few gulps and thanked the bartender. Monica was checking out the finger food so he joined several of his cousins and dropped into a chair. He swirled the ice in his glass and barely heard their conversation while his thoughts circled back to Abby.

When they'd been together, Abby told him that she wanted *everything*, the whole package in a lasting relationship: meaning, romance and a white knight. And she hadn't lied. To the contrary, he found out later that she'd wanted many white knights, not just him. When he found out about her unfaithfulness, it reminded him of his mother who had cheated on his father.

That was something Jack couldn't tolerate, something that made his stomach roll over whenever he thought about Abby's indiscretions, even two years after they'd broken up.

There was a time when he'd thought Abby the most beautiful, genuine, woman in the world and perfect for him.

She had always been hot in bed, demanding too, so perhaps that should have been a sign, an indicator that she couldn't be satisfied by just one man. While he'd sometimes been too busy to see her, while he worked twelve-hour days to acquire the money to buy and build a business, he had believed she was content. He thought they'd been happy, until he discovered evidence that he wasn't enough for her. That was something he couldn't live with. All he wanted after her betrayal was to be alone.

Later, he realized it was better to connect to someone cold, than to face another hurt down the road. He needed a woman who wouldn't lust after other men.

That worked in his relationship with Monica… for a while. Monica was the cold to Abby's hot. While Monica kept her personal appearance immaculate, her looks seemed to be her only interest beyond her next designer handbag or her next pair of shoes. Life had become routine with Monica, not hot and romantic. That suited Jack just fine after a life totally entwined with Abby's. But lately he wasn't so sure.

He was a realist, and no matter what Abby had said, he definitely knew fairytales did *not* happen. Abby had proved that.

Monica was a realist, too, and for a while they got along just fine, even if their life was a little bland. Monica didn't even mind his workaholic life.

While he'd never had the same feelings for her that he'd had for Abby, he and Monica were comfortable and that was probably a good thing. He never again wanted to go through the pain he'd experienced with Abby.

Monica had not demanded a lot from him or distracted him while he worked to buy back McAlister Construction.

She hadn't even pressured for them to move in together, although recently each time she visited him, she brought a few more of her things to his condo. As if she were slowly moving in. As if she thought theirs was more than the casual relationship Jack had thought he was getting into.

Unlike Abby who'd always been a handful, Monica demanded very little attention. Once, Monica had told him, 'I won't bother you when you're working. I don't care how hard you work because I want you to be successful.' That was well and good because he had worked himself to death these past four years, and even harder these last two years so he could buy back McAlister Construction, the family company his Uncle Peter had lost.

And working so hard had helped him forget Abby—though she still haunted his dreams.

Monica—who would become his *future wife* if she had her way—sashayed up to him and took a seat beside him at the large table. Her platinum-blond hair hung to just above her shoulders and she wore a low-cut white dress. While she sipped champagne, she gave him a sideways glance, her hazel eyes peering out beneath blunt cut bangs. Her freshly reddened lips curved into a smile, and it wasn't hard to read her thoughts. She thought this weekend and this wedding would seal the deal and convince him they should take the next step.

Uncomfortable, he ran his fingers around the inside of his collar, then noticed her face looked odd, a bit different. He frowned...trying to figure out what was different. Her forehead seemed a little frozen. He frowned again. Had she done something different with her makeup? Or had she gone under the knife again?

Yes, that was it.

And that was when he realized he hadn't really looked at her since he'd picked her up from her apartment that morning or during their flight to Ohio together. And he hadn't missed her during the five months while he'd been away.

Disturbing for a man who was considering tying the knot. He swirled his drink. The ice cubes rattled against the glass. This was not the first time Monica had plastic surgery. Although she'd denied it, breast implants weren't easy to hide.

Good Lord, Abby had such firm natural breasts. He remembered times he'd lowered his mouth to her nip—

"Jack, aren't you going to introduce me to your cousins?" Monica asked.

Glad to be distracted from of his thoughts, which had spiraled out of control again, Jack gazed at his girlfriend over his drink. "Sure." He cocked his head toward Alex. "Monica, this is my cousin, Alex Drake. Alex is an actor. He's from England and has just been offered a lead role in the U.S. We're all very proud of him."

Handsome Alex with his golden, movie-star good looks always made women swoon. He was an up-and-coming actor who appeared in several movies, but there was one downfall in his otherwise "golden" life: Five years ago, at twenty-two, Alex married a woman a decade older than him—an internationally renowned actress.

The family had one word for his wife Vanessa Caine—*bitch*. No, make that two words: *royal bitch*. Alex had been nothing more than her trophy. He was now separated and he was fighting to legally get out of the marriage.

Next in the introductions, Jack swept his hand toward the cousin who resembled him the most because of their dark hair coloring. Trent.

"This is Trent Farrington. His grandfather, James, is the owner of Farrington Enterprises and Construction."

Jack noticed Monica's eyes brightened. "James Farrington—the *billionaire*?" she gushed.

"Yes." Trent's dark eyes narrowed.

Jack hoped Monica wouldn't say more because Trent disliked gold diggers and that's what Monica appeared to be at the moment. "Trent's grandfather bought and restored the McAlister estate after one of my uncles had to sell. His grandfather, my Uncle James, is our host for this house party and the wedding."

"Which uncle had to sell? You mentioned you have several."

"It was my Uncle Peter." Jack indicated his uncle on the other side of the room, but didn't go into details with Monica.

The family all knew Uncle Peter had let the estate run to ruin and was going to sell the house to a developer who planned to tear it down. Uncle James stepped in and bought the place. Then there were other issues before that, because of mismanagement, his Uncle Peter had lost the construction company to an outside buyer. They owned the business for a short time, and now Jack had bought back the company and was bringing it back into the family.

His Uncle Peter saw himself as the eternal player and ladies' man. At forty-something, he had curling brown hair—still not gray—and with his dark-rimmed glasses, he brought to mind one of those old-time movie stars. Peter had some charm, but he'd been spoiled most of his life. Unfortunately, common sense was not his strong suit.

At this moment, Uncle Peter was cozying up on a sofa

next to a redhead who appeared a decade older than himself. Judging by her demeanor and chic accessories, she had money.

Jack raised his glass in another cousin's direction and continued his introductions around the table. "This is my cousin Chris McAlister, from Australia. He has a brother who isn't here, but they could pass for identical twins." Chris was more golden in looks, like Alex. "So, Monica, we're from all around the globe."

Jack indicated with his thumb toward another dark-haired cousin across the room that leaned against the fireplace mantle. "That is Tristan Knight, a very successful New York doctor. He's also a bit of a workaholic."

"Like you?" Monica leaned toward him and her lips curved. "That's okay. The harder you work, Jack, the more money I'll have to spend." Then she eyed all the guys. When no one responded or paid her any attention—and Monica was used to attention—she shrugged and said, "It was nice to meet you all. Excuse me. I'm going to the ladies' room."

After she left, Jack glanced around the table at his cousins. "So what's going on?"

"We were going to ask you the same thing," Trent said dryly. "But it seems obvious. It looks like you could be next in line, Jack. You're all dropping like flies. I'd say we, but I plan to avoid the curse."

"Did I say I was getting married?" Jack asked through tight lips.

Trent lifted his glass. "That's the rumor flying around the family for the past month, that you're about to become engaged to Ms. Monica Stevens. I'd say it's your funeral, Jack. Frankly, I'm happy it's not me. I'm warning you that marriage is for *fools*. Most women aren't in it for love."

Frowning past Jack's head, Alex folded his arms over his chest. "Looks like Tristan might be set to make a fool out of himself as well, and even sooner than you, Jack."

They all glanced across the room to their cousin Tristan as his fiancée slithered up to him and put her arms around his waist.

Jack shrugged. "I don't know, Alex. She's a pretty girl. What is there to be a fool about? Maybe they'll be happy."

"You think so?" Alex blew out a deep breath. "I met Tristan's fiancé on the upstairs landing. She stopped me, put her hand on my chest, then slipped her card into my jacket pocket. She told me that if I was ever in New York to look her up for tea, then she moved on. I don't know if wearing my wedding ring keeps them away or attracts them. I felt like some kind of stud service. That she thought I would be someone safe and discreet. I don't think his fiancée has any idea that Tristan and I are cousins."

Trent blew out a deep breath and slumped back in his chair. "Marriage *is* for fools. So what can we do? We can't say anything to him. Like the rest of us, Tristan won't appreciate any interference in his life."

Alex shoved his chair away from the table and rose to his feet. "Bloody hell. And I'm one of the *married* fools. I should have listened to you, Trent—about marriage—before I met my own doom." Alex turned and walked away.

"He doesn't look too happy," Jack muttered as he watched Alex's retreating back.

Trent leaned across the table. "Can you blame him? His wife is a damn shrew. If things go well for him, he'll be divorced soon though. He feels she won't let that happen, however, unless she gets a bundle—of his money. That's another issue about marriage for some of us. We have to watch for gold diggers. Don't suppose you have to worry about that, Jack. I'm assuming Monica is well off herself?"

Jack raised an eyebrow. "Not really. Her dad works hard as a dentist, but they're not rich."

"So that explains why she has such perfect teeth," Chris interjected, in his Australian accent, and with a sardonic curve of his mouth.

Although Jack had at one time seen a few of Monica's early childhood photos and suspected at least her teeth were capped, he ignored Chris's comment and changed the subject.

"I'm doing well in my business now," Jack said, narrowing his eyes, "but it's been a hard, uphill climb."

Chris swirled the ice in his drink, a slight smirk on his lips. "I was surprised when you and Abby broke up. Is she here for the wedding? From what I remembered she was beautiful, delightful—and a friend of Carly's. And now that she's no longer with you, I'm wondering—"

"Abby's not coming this weekend. Carly would have told me," Jack grumbled.

Chris gave Jack a pointed look. "If she were, would it matter? It's been at least two years since you dated her. If she does come this week, would you mind if I talked her up?"

Jack didn't want to draw any attention to why he still cared after two years, but he did. Anger and hurt still rose in him when he thought of Abby.

"I couldn't care less," Jack lied, grinding the words through his teeth. "It's all *water under the bridge* with us."

Trent's brows jerked together. "Did you break up with Abby because she wrecked your new car?"

Jack's shoulders bunching, he clamped his arms across

his chest. "I spent years saving money for that car and it was expensive and special, but, no, that's not the reason. I'm not that shallow."

Chris leaned in closer. "Jack, you didn't break up with her because your laptop was in the trunk of your car, with your work on it? Work you hadn't backed up? Didn't you lose a client because of that? I remember you were really upset."

Jack narrowed his eyes. "I was upset, but no. That wasn't the issue either."

Chris leaned back in his chair and gaped. "I can't imagine why you broke up with Abby then. I know some women can be traitors, but she seemed loyal. Anyway, what do I know? I met one devious woman who needs a payback for what she did to me, so I won't trust another woman enough to marry anytime soon either. However Abby..." Chris raised an eyebrow. "I wouldn't mind getting to know her better if she's here alone these next four days. As long as you don't mind, Jack?"

Just the thought of his handsome cousin from Australia, looking like a golden Viking prince with his slightly longish hair, hitting on his ex-girlfriend Abby, made Jack's blood rise in temperature.

"I'm sure Abby won't be here this weekend," Jack ground out. He blew out a deep breath. He recalled the woman who'd dropped the flowers. He frowned. When he'd told Carly on the phone he could make the wedding, he had asked Carly pointblank if Abby would be attending, but that day they'd had a bad connection… He was sure Carly had reassured him through the static on the line that Abby would not be here.

Jack changed the subject. "How's your brother, Chris?"

"He's off on one of his expeditions, this time in the wilds of South America. Too busy to catch a plane or to even discuss this event. Weddings aren't his style either."

Jack nodded. "Doesn't seem to be the style of any of us."

"And your brothers, Jack? Are they coming?" Chris asked.

"Two should be here in time for the wedding. That's all of us, except Nick… And who knows when he's coming back, *maybe never.* Nick doesn't keep in touch, and he left abruptly."

Uncle James Farrington, the self-appointed patriarch of the family, strode toward the table. The older man looked sophisticated in a tux. Despite his age, he had a full head of wavy gray hair and sparkling blue eyes.

Jack noticed that two of his elderly great-great aunts who traipsed by, cast Mr. James Farrington allover admiring glances.

His aunts then glanced at Jack and his cousins at the table. "I've never seen so many handsome men in one room," Aunt Gertrude said, louder than she expected and all the men chuckled as they passed.

Her sister, Aunt Beatrice, pulled her along by the elbow. "Oh, don't be naughty, Gertrude. And besides, somewhere along the line they're your distant nephews."

"Not James though—and I caught you looking, too, Beatrice," Aunt Gertrude muttered as they walked away.

Trent stood. "Grandpa, can I get you a chair?"

"No, you all keep talking," the older man said. "I'm only checking in before I make my rounds to visit the other guests. So how are my boys?"

Alex caught the question as he returned with a drink in

his hand. "Fine."

After everyone gave Uncle James an update on how they were, Jack added, "Thanks for hosting the wedding for Carly."

"You're all my beloved wife's nephews. I consider you all part of my family and dear to me." Uncle James glanced at the oil painting of his wife above the fireplace mantle. "Eliza meant the world to me."

They all swiveled their heads to look at the portrait of Uncle James's wife. Eliza McAlister Farrington looked regal in a blue ball gown and a glittering diamond tiara.

Uncle James put his hand on his grandson Trent's shoulder. "If only she knew our line might end with Trent here. My poor dear Eliza would be heartbroken. So I hold out hope that this wedding will give my grandson ideas."

Trent gave his grandfather a wry smile. "Perhaps just the opposite. I'm sure there will be some drama this weekend to put me off marriage for at least another five years."

"Well, boys," James Farrington said with a gleam in his eyes, "I've told Trent his time to get married is running out, but he thinks I'm joking. As the last of the Farringtons, he has to take responsibility and carry the name forward. It's his duty to procreate."

"Something like a horse used for stud?" Trent muttered.

Around the table, Jack's cousins all chuckled.

Mr. James Farrington whipped a steely gaze at his grandson. "However you get it done, Trent, as long as it's in wedlock," he said in a cool tone. "I don't go for having babies without marriage, or none of this 'shacking up' young people do these days." He looked around the table at his nephews. "I recommend you all get married, like Alex here."

Alex paled, then he gulped his drink.

"Traditional family values have always been important to me," Uncle James continued. "Marriage is for your happiness and to have children." This was something they'd all heard over the years, especially his grandson Trent. Perhaps that was why Trent tended to run the opposite way at the mere mention of marriage.

For Trent's sake, Jack changed the conversation once again. "The estate looks great, Uncle James."

"It's been a labor of love, so I'm glad you think so, Jack," his uncle said. "And it's your family homestead. I want it preserved for future generations of McAlister descendants."

Jack nodded. "You have. You've saved and restored the estate from rack and ruin—well beyond restored—and the improvements you've made are amazing."

Located outside greater Cincinnati, Ohio, the estate still maintained five hundred acres that his Uncle Peter hadn't sold off to finance gambling ventures. The house was filled with family antiques and artifacts from over the years.

"That's the least I can do for the McAlister line. I want it to stay in the family for the entire clan."

"That's generous of you, Uncle James," Alex said.

"That's not all, boys. I have something else important to say. I've received word someone is upset about our little family gathering. There could be trouble this weekend and I want you to be on the alert. I've learned that with advantages come disadvantages… Before you ask, just know I've received several anonymous threats…"

Jack frowned.

Uncle James gave them a pointed look. "It's probably nothing. However, since someone might think this wedding's a good opportunity to do damage to this family, or to me, I need you boys to keep your eyes and ears open for anything unusual. I'd appreciate it and so will the bride and groom."

Jack straightened his shoulders. "This sounds serious. Should we hire additional security?"

"I have."

"Do you think it's because I'm taking over McAlister Construction?"

"Possibly," the older man agreed. "Burns Construction and Preston Construction might feel threatened. Ralph Preston is my friend and I'm not really worried because his business seems strong. However, Ansen Burns has always been a big hot shot with an equally big temper and he's been known to resort to shady management practices. He might be angry because I loaned you some of the money and he wanted to buy McAlister. He wouldn't do the dirty work himself, but he might hire someone. So, while there is probably nothing to worry about, I am concerned enough about this that I want you all to be on the alert for signs of trouble this week.

All the cousins said they would.

Uncle James gave them a brief smile. "Not to worry too much. I think the weekend will be uneventful. But I must also mention that I've noticed your Uncle Peter acting strange."

"Uncle Peter is strange," Trent chimed in.

They all threw a glance over at Uncle Peter who flapped his arms like a chicken and looked to be telling a silly joke to the redheaded woman he'd been spending time with that evening.

Uncle James sighed. "It wasn't easy for him to lose

everything." Then he changed the subject. "We have a lot of activities planned this long weekend. There will be boating and other water sports. I want you to enjoy the grounds, the house, the pool, and all the amenities, so make yourselves at home—this is your home. Many of our guests are staying at the hotel nearby, but you've all been placed in your usual bedrooms in the family wing, here at the house."

Uncle James added, "Several singers and bands will also be housed here over the weekend too. "Perhaps, Alex, you wouldn't mind singing a few songs for us, too?"

Alex was a talented musician and singer as well as an actor. The corners of Alex's mouth turned up. "I'd be happy to."

"All right, boys, I'll see you later."

After Uncle James walked away, Jack leaned across the table toward his cousins and said, "In spite of his reassurance that there's nothing to worry about, we need to be vigilant and on the lookout for trouble."

Trent swirled the drink in his hand. "Yeah, you're right."

The movement of the kitchen door swinging open caught Jack's attention. He caught another glimpse of the woman he'd seen earlier. She stood at the kitchen island, talking to Carly.

"*Abby…*" Jack murmured on the exhale. There was no mistake this time. She *was* here!

Trent also caught sight of Abby and crossed his arms over his chest, smiling broadly. "I guess you were wrong about Abby not coming?"

"Yeah, *wrong...*" Jack said in a low voice.

Chris flicked Jack an amused glance. "Since you broke up with her a long time ago, mate, do you mind…? If she's solo this weekend, could any of us—?"

"Absolutely *not*," Jack snapped. "You are my cousins, and if you hit on Abby, I will make you regret it."

"For someone who is supposed to be over a girl, bloody hell, you sure don't act like it," Alex said matter-of-factly.

Jack nearly growled. "You are to stay away from her, all right?" He looked around the table at all his male cousins. Each one gave him a nod of agreement. However, he didn't miss the knowing glances that passed between them. "Don't look that way. It's for your own sake," he warned.

"*Our sake*?" Chris asked, rising from his chair. "If that's the case, I can look after myself. I'm sure you don't mind if I take the risk myself."

Jack pinned him with an icy glance. "Abby is off limits. I mean it. There *should* be some kind of cousins' code, if there isn't one in place already."

"I'll do my best," Chris said, with a mischievous twinkle in his eyes. He sat back down. "But you're laying claim to two of the prettiest women here. I call that royally unfair."

His heart still pounding from seeing Abby, Jack ignored the comment as his mind raced to come up with a plan. He clenched his teeth and decided that he'd be casual and cool when he faced her. Now, that his initial shock had passed, the last words they'd had, ground in his stomach like stones at a mill.

Two years ago, Abby had called from her European trip with her family to tell him that she was pregnant—in spite of taking birth control pills. She admitted she'd missed a few pills, but had thought that wouldn't matter too much. He remembered the anger he had felt at the time, but he had been under enormous pressure. *She* had known how hard he worked to build up his money so that he could buy a business, but she had been careless and 'slipped up.' How does someone screw up something like that? At the time, he'd not been in a position to start a family. A setback like that would have ruined his chances to succeed. While he hadn't hid the anger and disappointment he felt, he'd done the right thing and had asked her to marry him.

Then, before she could answer, feeling trapped, he had told her that if they *really* were having a baby, they'd marry in a quick, quiet affair—not the big wedding of her dreams.

"Do you think I'd lie to you about something like this?" she'd asked, sounding affronted.

He'd regretted how he'd spoken to her, but it reminded him of all the responsibilities he'd shouldered, raising his younger brothers, while his mother was out running around. It was in his nature—he liked things to be planned—not thrown at him.

Over the next few days, he'd come to terms with it though, and went shopping for a baby gift to show Abby he was okay with whatever happened. He would handle the extra responsibility and still succeed in his business plans. And he had been fine, until three days later, when he went to drop off a present for Abby and the baby at her apartment. That visit changed everything. He'd discovered that the baby disrupting their lives might not even be his.

Monica was her roommate at the time and had acted weird when she opened the door, as if she were protecting Abby, and that made him suspicious. 'You can put that in her room, Jack." But when he started down the hallway, she'd quickly said, "Oh, no, never mind. Maybe I'd better do that for you. I don't think Abby would want you in her room while she's not here.' As she spoke she'd glanced nervously over her shoulder toward the room.

'Why not?' His jealousy had roared to life and he'd persisted. 'What are you hiding from me, Monica? Is it something about Abby?'

Monica reluctantly let him into Abby's bedroom. 'I don't want to do this, Jack. I don't want to see you hurt,' she'd said.

When he entered the bedroom, Jack saw the incriminating evidence with his own eyes: Another man's jacket hung in Abby's closet, folded men's shirts lay on her dresser, a razor sat on her sink, and several pairs of boxers had been carelessly thrown into the hamper in her bathroom.

Monica had watched him as he strode around and took in all the items, shaking her head as if embarrassed for him.

"I suppose you have a right to know, but I don't know if I should be the one...," Monica had said.

"What is it?" he had asked through gritted teeth.

Then Monica showed him pictures—pictures of Abby with Vince Michaels on Abby's social page. "I think she only sees him once in awhile, Jack... It's probably doesn't mean that much to her... I don't want to be the one to bear this bad news to you—"

"Monica, you don't ever have to cover for Abby again," Jack said as he stalked out of the apartment with his present.

After that, he'd called and interrupted Abby's European fun and broke up with her. He wouldn't date or marry a cheater, and if she were pregnant, he needed to be certain he was the father before offering support.

"I'm not ready for marriage," he had told her. "I want a DNA test. I'll pay for the baby's support and yours—if tests show the baby is mine."

"Is that how you think of me, Jack?" Abby had asked.

He remembered the hurt in her voice. Afterwards, she had not slammed down the phone as he expected. She'd just quietly disconnected.

He didn't call her back. That was the last time he spoke to her, but he had been sure she'd have called him back if she really thought he was the father. So, he waited. She never called and neither did he.

Six months later, he ran into Abby at a party. By then, Monica was clinging to his arm and there had been no chance to speak to Abby. She'd looked as slim as a woman could. Had she terminated the pregnancy as Monica suspected after hearing a rumor? It also proved the baby probably wasn't his, or she would have let him have a DNA test, and insisted he marry her. The other possibility was that she'd never been pregnant at all, and she had been setting a trap.

He felt like he didn't know Abby at all.

Jack rose from his chair after deciding to confront Abby instead of waiting to run into her. "I'll be back."

He headed into the kitchen and stood right across from her. She looked panicky when she first saw him, but quickly composed herself.

"So I see you *are* here," he accused.

The woman, who had cut out his heart, thrown it to the ground, then stomped on it hard, now appeared as fresh as the newly bloomed pink roses outside the mansion. Her clear ivory skin, and the shine in her long sun-streaked hair, spoke of good health.

His gaze roved over her breasts that swelled over the low neckline of her violet dress, then down her slender legs to her dainty feet encased in high-heeled sandals. Nothing had changed about the way she looked, other than there was no warmth in her expression. Even so, she was as beautiful as ever standing there next to his cousin.

Suddenly, he was too close to her and had to get away.

The blood drained from her face. "Jack!" Abby whispered.

"Jack," Carly sputtered, "we're just making sure the staff has the menu all lined up for the entertainment this weekend, and for the reception. We didn't expect you to arrive yet."

"Really, Carly?" he drawled.

"Ouch," Abby cried. Careless, she'd sliced herself with the kitchen shears. Blood spurted from her finger.

Jack jumped into action. He grabbed a paper towel, took Abby's hand in his, and wound the towel around her finger to stop the bleeding. How dainty her hand appeared in his as her familiar fragrance wafted in the air surrounding them…

"Are you all right?" Jack asked hoarsely. "I didn't mean to startle you." He couldn't believe *he* was apologizing to *her*. In addition, he damned well knew he didn't want to be this close and to have the memories her scent evoked, spiraling around his heart, once again binding him to her like a chain.

"You remember Abby?" Carly asked with an innocent face.

"Yes," he said through tight lips.

Carly knew damned well he *knew* Abby—and in the biblical sense. She should have warned him Abby would be here before he made arrangements to come early and remain here so long. He'd speak to Carly about that later.

"I didn't expect you either." Abby's hand trembled in his, and she avoided looking at his face, which indicated she also hadn't wanted to see him—probably just as much as he didn't want to see her. Fleetingly, in a moment of weakness, he wondered if she was still seeing Vince Michaels.

"I'm sorry if it's my fault that you cut yourself."

"It's not, Jack. It's nothing. I'm okay."

While one of the staff members took over and put a bandage on Abby's finger, Jack asked her why she was there.

"I'm the Maid of Honor."

"I'm the *Best Man*," he informed her dryly. He narrowed his eyes and flicked a gaze to Carly. "Was this a plot to throw us together, Carly? If it was, you've wasted your time… Why don't you concentrate on your own life?"

"Jack, *please*. You're being Best Man was only settled last minute, remember? At first you said you couldn't come, so you're making a big deal about nothing," Carly rattled on. "It's my wedding. I want my best friend here—and my cousin. Now why don't you go on out there? Abby and I will be out in a minute to join everyone."

Jack gave Carly a curt nod and left the kitchen with apprehension still swirling in his gut and still a little disturbed that he'd flustered Abby. So much so, that she'd cut herself just because she'd seen him.

Several minutes later, Carly and Abby strode out of the kitchen and joined his group of cousins.

Carly beamed a smile. "Well Jack has already been reacquainted with Abby, but do the rest of you remember her? Some of you must have met Abby before."

Jack introduced the cousins that Abby hadn't met before. In the middle of the introductions, Monica sashayed up to the table and linked her arm with Jack's.

"Monica, do you remember, Abby?" Carly asked, too sweetly.

Monica's eyes narrowed. She tightened her fingers on

Jack's elbow. "How could I forget Abby? You know we were once roommates, Carly. Hello, Abby. It's been awhile."

Jack noticed the shadows deepen in Abby's pretty aqua-blue eyes. "Yes, it has been," she said in a low voice. "I hope you're doing well."

Was she sincere?

All Jack wanted in that moment was to ask her what the hell had happened to them: *Why, Abby? Why did you cheat on me?* He'd been so attracted to her, and until he found out about Vince and the others, he thought she was in love with him. Even now, he could feel the almost electrical quality that sizzled like a live wire between them. His attraction to her was still there.

As if by instinct, he reached out his hand to touch her but caught himself before he made a real fool of himself.

Carly smiled up at him. "Jack, since you're the Best Man, and Abby is the Maid of Honor, it looks like you two will be paired together a bit this weekend."

Monica pursed her lips and narrowed her eyes. "I hope not too much. I hate to be away from my *fiancé* for long. That's what it's like when you're in love."

Abby's face fell at the mention of fiancé. "I-I see… I hope you'll both be happy… Excuse me I remember something I have to do in the kitchen." With that, Abby strode away.

Carly frowned. "Excuse me, too." She followed Abby into the kitchen.

Jack took Monica aside, a little perturbed at her. "Our engagement is not official," he whispered. "Nothing has been formally decided between us. I've been gone for five months. You presume too much… After this weekend, we need to discuss whether or not it is a good idea to get engaged."

Monica gave him a brief smile. "Sorry, Jack, I couldn't help myself. I know you might feel a bit rushed, but I love you so much. I just want to make sure Abby knows that you and I are together."

CHAPTER THREE

Abby stepped into the elegant ballroom. Glittering chandeliers soared above on the high ceiling. Numerous round tables with white tablecloths, flowers, and candles, were placed about the enormous room. On one wall, French doors led to a stone patio, pool, lawns, flower gardens, and steps that lead down to the lake. On the other side, a large stage was setup for several entertainments that were scheduled throughout the week.

Abby spotted Jack and Monica sitting together at one of the dinner tables. *They were getting married!* Abby's heart ached with an inner despair as she headed for the other side of the room. When she found a vacant seat at another table, she sighed in relief, thankful she wouldn't have to speak to them that evening.

However, during the meal, Abby couldn't stop her eyes from wandering to where they sat. *Jack must be really happy to want to marry Monica.* Tears burned the backs of her eyes, but Abby managed to maintain her composure throughout dinner. She immersed herself in the lively conversation at the table.

After dinner, Abby left the ballroom, tired of keeping her fake smile in place all evening. She sought refuge in her pretty, colonial-style bedroom at the mansion. She threw herself on the comfortable four-poster bed and let all her emotions burst free.

Silent tears flowed as Abby pressed her hands to her cheeks. She faced the facts: Jack had broken up with her to be with her roommate. Although she tried to forget him, she couldn't stop all those painful memories from surfacing now that she'd seen him again.

Abby sniffled and grabbed several tissues from the nightstand. *Damn.* Jack still got to her. From the first time she'd seen him, years ago, she'd thought he was her soul mate, the love of her life. And it had been love at first sight for her, just hadn't been the same for him.

Why can't I move on too?

When morning arrived, Abby decided she'd cried enough over a man who didn't love her. She wouldn't hide in her room and ruin her entire weekend or tarnish these events for her best friend. This was Carly's wedding celebration and memories of these days would shine for the rest of Carly's life…if she didn't ruin it.

She would just ignore Jack and Monica. Hello and good-bye would be the extent of her conversation with either of them. The only reason she'd broken down the night before was because it had been such a shock to see them here as a couple.

She could do this, and she *had* to forget this man who didn't love her. Maybe that's what she needed all along…to see Jack again, to feel this pain, and then she'd finally get over him.

* * *

Several boats were going out on the lake, so after a quick breakfast with the other bridesmaids, Abby stepped out into the sunshine and headed for the docks. She was determined to enjoy all the activities at this fabulous mansion before the wedding.

When she arrived at the shore, the water stretched in the distance and sparkled a brilliant blue.

Mr. James Farrington waved her over and quickly escorted her by the elbow across the wooden dock to a sleek and sporty, open vessel.

Trent sat at the helm with one hand on the steering wheel. As she scanned the group already on board, Abby's heart sank to her toes. Seated at the back of the boat, Jack and Monica lounged on the wrap-around bench.

Mr. James Farrington beamed at Abby. "There you go, dear," he said, handing Abby onto the boat. "You know Jack and Monica. You're all old friends I hear. And I do believe you said you were single. Why don't you sit here, next to my grandson? Trent is single as well."

Trent's grandpa wasn't going to take no for an answer and waved his hand, signaling her toward the control panel where the captain's seat could sit two people romantically.

Trent's friendly expression stilled and grew serious. "I just remembered something I have to do at the house. You will excuse me, Abby?" He turned to Jack. "Do you mind driving the boat? I'll take in another ride on the lake later."

"All right." Jack moved to the bench at the helm to take over the controls. Of course, Monica joined him.

Abby's cheeks burned. Trent had walked away like she was poison. Had Jack said something bad about her to Trent? No…she couldn't believe Jack would do that to her.

Mr. James Farrington threw out his hands in frustration, then stalked toward the house, following his grandson.

With a pleasant smile, Sam Preston strode across the dock toward the boat, looking to board before it left the dock. Abby's nerves tensed when she recognized him. She didn't expect him to arrive until later in the week.

"Hey, Jack," Sam called out, "I just got here. I haven't seen you in years. Can I catch a ride with you?"

"Sure," Jack said.

Sam hopped on the boat. "I'm glad to see you, Abby," he said with a warm look in his brown eyes. Of medium build, he had a smattering of freckles on his face and dark reddish-brown hair. "Why don't we sit back here? I hoped we'd have a chance to talk."

She reluctantly sat at the bench at the back of the boat with him.

Jack cleared his throat, catching their attention. "Sam," he said, nodding in Monica's direction. "This is Monica Stevens."

"*Happy* to meet you, Sam," Monica said in a glib voice. "Especially since you seem to be such a *good friend* of Abby's."

Abby winced. If she ever decided to consider Sam seriously as someone to date, she didn't want to do so in front of Monica's prying eyes.

Sam turned his attention back to Abby. "You are as beautiful as ever, Abby."

Her face heated at his compliment. "Thank you."

Abby was surprised, when, on his way to untie the boat from the dock, Jack shot her a surly, sideways glance.

Anger sizzled inside her. *What was that supposed to mean?* She was the injured party in their relationship. He got what he wanted. Monica.

Jack scowled at her again, returned to the console, and turned the ignition. The engines rumbled to life. The boat jerked away from the dock. Abby gripped the seat to steady herself, wishing she hadn't come, especially with the way Jack had looked at her—as if he blamed her for everything.

The waterway glistened before them. The sun warmed Abby's skin and was refreshing after the piles of snow and the colder-than-normal winter and spring they'd had.

When she glanced up, Monica had her arm draped around Jack's waist as he steered the boat.

Jealousy slammed Abby. She jerked her attention back toward the shore lined with pines and maple trees. After all this time, why was she bothered seeing the two of them together? Jack had become Monica's boyfriend only three months after he'd broken up with Abby. She had known that because, a few months into their relationship, Monica had called Abby to let her know.

At that time, Monica had said she wasn't gloating, but that she'd called Abby just to check in and gauge her feelings for the situation. "I hope you don't mind that Jack and I are seeing each other? I wanted to make sure you weren't too hurt."

Awash with pain, Abby had choked out a lie. "N-no, no, why should I be hurt? We broke up."

"Well, I told you how he was, remember? And you knew he liked me, so it was expected, wasn't it?"

Yeah, Abby thought as she glanced at them now. When they were roommates, Monica had often told her how Jack had flirted with her when she wasn't looking or when they were alone. Even then, Monica had asked if Abby was jealous. However, Abby had been deeply crushed when she heard they were together. But enough of that…

It was a beautiful day to be on the water.

She couldn't see Jack's face as he steered the boat, but she saw that Monica still leaned against him, her breast brushing his arm.

Abby sighed and settled in the seat. *I'm okay with them being together. It's much better to have found out I'd been nothing special to him.*

Abby lifted her chin. She was glad to have found out that he wasn't loyal. And good riddance, considering the way he had broken up with her after she'd shared the scary news that she was pregnant. He'd been upset, then deserted her to handle the pregnancy on her own and gone in search of greener pastures. He had let her suffer alone.

Although she suspected he didn't cheat on her while they were dating, Jack must have been unable to contain his attraction for her ex-roommate. A twinge of pain hit Abby again because he had preferred the *perfect* Monica.

Abby pulled her hat low over her forehead and sighed. Her mistake today was that she didn't jump ship when Trent did. Good grief, was she a glutton for punishment?

They cruised on the lake for about a mile, when another boat headed toward them, speeding and throwing out a huge wake of water in its path.

Abby's heart pounded and she gripped the seat when she realized the boat could hit them head-on.

At the last minute, Jack pulled to the side and let the maniac drive by. The man raised his hat in salute.

"Damn it. It's Uncle Peter," Jack grumbled. "What the hell?"

Monica had her hands clenched on the back of the chair. "Was he trying to kill us?"

Jack shook his head. "No, Uncle Peter is harmless. He's probably showing off a bit for this woman he's been hanging out with here."

"He doesn't look harmless to me," Monica muttered.

Jack kept on driving. "It was crazy of him, but maybe he's just blowing off steam. I'll have a talk with him. He has no reason to be angry with me, and I don't even know if he knew that was us. I don't think it was personal."

"Looked like he was furious to me when he passed us, Jack," Monica said.

Abby tried to relax as she released her grip on the seat cushion.

"Are you okay, Abby?" Sam asked.

"Yeah." She was just glad the crazy uncle was far away now.

When they approached the destination island, relief and apprehension swept her. Now, she'd have to endure a picnic lunch alone with Jack, Monica, and Sam.

Ten minutes later, Jack gently glided the boat onto the shore of a hilly and thickly wooded island.

"The island belongs to the estate, and is uninhabited," he explained. "There is a cabin on the other side, which hasn't been used in years. The estate owns several miles of lakefront."

When the boat's bow was beached on the muddy shoreline, Jack said, "By the marks already on the shore, it looks like someone else has been here recently. Perhaps Uncle Peter."

A sign further up from the beach read: Private, no Trespassing.

Monica leaned into Jack and let her fingers play with the hair at his temple. "I'm glad we've arrived. And I've had such a nice time so far, Jack. I am really enjoying your family. They've all been so welcoming to me, as if we were already married."

Abby clenched her teeth. Wanting to get off the boat

quickly, she jumped from the side, and one foot sank into the muddier part of the beach.

"Darn it," Abby muttered.

Sam leaped to a dryer part of the shore. "Mind if I help?" He took her hand and pulled her out of the sucking mud.

Once on dry land, Abby tugged her hand free from his. "Thanks, Sam."

Not to be put off, Sam looped his arm around her and helped her get settled on a nearby log. When he bent and slipped off her shoe she had an uncomfortable feeling he was too close.

She grew even more uncomfortable when she glanced into his adoring eyes.

"I'm glad you're here, Abby. While we have a moment alone, I want your answer. Will you go out with me again?" He lowered his voice. "I don't want to be the nice guy who finishes last in this race."

Abby blew out a breath. "I'm thinking about it."

Sam gave her a nod. "All right. I won't push you." He washed the mud off her shoe in the water.

Why can't I just give him a chance? They'd gone on two casual dates, one to the Cincinnati Zoo and the other to the art museum. On those dates, she'd kept him at a distance though—as a friend only. He was a pleasant man, the 'nice guy' as he had said. He was attractive enough, but still, something held her back. Maybe because he had been the guy down the street when she was growing up, and her brother's friend, she wasn't physically attracted to Sam. However, she'd always known he had a *thing* for her.

And then there was *Jack*. Like a phantom, he'd stood in the way of any other relationship for her and had always been at the back of her mind, even though they'd broken up. *She was crazy!*

Abby gritted her teeth and watched Jack help Monica off the bow of the boat. He carried her and set her down on the drier part of the beach.

Jack being so close with Monica was all Abby needed to make her decision. This weekend she was going to give Sam a chance—a real chance.

Seeing Jack again was affecting her, and not in a good way… She needed a diversion. Her problem was she'd never been able to look past Jack, no matter how much she wanted to move on.

While Monica walked on past, Jack paused for a second by Abby and said for her ears only, "How fitting for you, Abby. You're no damsel in distress, but the *act* must earn you points with men."

Abby gaped at him, anger sizzling inside her. "I am not—"

"Don't deny it." The cold hard look in his green eyes stopped her. He stalked past Abby. "Monica," he barked, "let's explore the island."

Monica set her bag on the ground. "Do you mind if we don't, Jack? I didn't bring the proper shoes for walking. Why don't you bring out the chairs so I can work on my tan? We can catch up on old times with Abby. It has been so long." She sent a sweet smile Abby's way. "Wouldn't you like that?"

Abby flushed. She didn't want to catch up on anything with either of them. Besides, there was nothing to say. She didn't blame Monica for wanting Jack. *He* was the *one* who had made the decision to split up. It was *him* who preferred the perfect Monica.

Just look at her. She must use a ton of hairspray. There

wasn't a hair out of place—unlike Abby's own, which was escaping her ponytail and springing loose around her face.

Abby sighed. "No, thanks, Monica. Maybe later. I am going for a walk. I hear there is a nice view from the top of the hill."

At Sam's bright smile, Abby winced.

"Of course," he said, "and we can be alone. I'll go with you."

"Be careful with her, Sam," Jack said dryly. "Abby sometimes lands herself into trouble and drags others in with her."

Abby gritted her teeth. She'd had enough of Jack McAlister and his comments.

"Jack, I don't know what you're referring to," Abby snapped back. "And since we no longer *know* each other—and we haven't seen each other in two years—why don't you keep your opinions to yourself?"

Abby stormed off through the brush and up the hill. She really wanted to be alone...with herself, not even Sam at this point.

"Wait for me," Sam called out.

Jack yelled from behind her, "Abby! One of those trails can be..."

Abby didn't hear the rest and didn't wait. She trudged on, wanting to get away from everyone. When she reached a fork in the path, she had to choose one. Abby decided on the most secluded trail, to get away from everyone. And she might as well walk to see the view. She chose one that looked to climb to higher terrain.

Abby hiked farther. When she glanced over her shoulder, to her surprise, she found not Sam, but Jack striding behind her, which only made her pace faster. What was he doing, taking a walk without his precious Monica?

I can't believe I'm letting Jack get to me. Abby muttered something rude under her breath. *How dare he say I drag others into trouble—*

A branch slapped her in the face. "Argghhhhhhh," she cried out as barbed branches grabbed at her clothes. Once clear of them, she glanced over her shoulder again to see if Jack was laughing at her.

"Abby, wait," Jack shouted. "Watch out!"

Her next step didn't find solid ground. Abby let out a yelp. With heart pounding, she slid downward. She landed on her butt and went down the slick muddy path as if it were a slide. She hit the bottom, twisted her ankle, and landed flat on her back.

Abby lay there, stunned, staring at the trees and the blue sky overhead.

Jack was standing above her at the top of the thirty-foot hill. "Are you hurt?" he asked, alarmed. He made his way down a long winding path and beat his way through the bushes with a stick to reach her. Tall and handsome, he hovered over her, his black hair gleaming in the sun.

"Abby, are you all right? *Answer me!*"

Pain shot through her and she sat up. "Yeah." Her ankle hurt, and her rear end and hip stung, but otherwise she seemed okay.

"See, I told you you'd land yourself in some kind of trouble. I came after you because I was afraid you'd take this path and kill yourself. I tried to warn you some of the paths might be dangerous, but you didn't wait to hear. You never were cautious... Never listened."

"*Not cautious?* And no wonder I don't want to *listen* to you," Abby blurted out. She shook a finger at him. "But you *listen* to me, Jack. No matter what you think of me, or how much you dislike me, don't make comments about me in front of other people—or in front of me. We are no longer *acquainted*. I'll wait here for Sam. He'll come and help me."

Jack grinned slightly and ignored her rant. "I saw Sam heading off on one of the other paths," he said more softly. "He probably wasn't aware which path you took, so you're going to have to accept my help. Lucky, or unlucky for you, I played here as a kid. I know the island well." Jack extended his palm. "Are you sure you're all right? But I'm not sure why *I* even care." He muttered the last under his breath but she heard him.

Tears blurred her eyes and she tried to keep her feelings about his painful comment to herself. "Jack, you don't have to worry about me. I'm okay," she said through tight lips. "Just go on. I'll find my way back in a minute."

He stuck his hand out again. There was nothing else she could do…

Though she hated that she needed his help, she took his hand. When she stood and put pressure on her foot, she winced. Yes, her ankle hurt, and her backside and hip stung, but nothing like the ache in her heart.

When he tried to steady her, an electrical attraction zipped through her. Abby shook off his hand and shied away. "How do we get out of here?"

"This way. The incline is more gradual. We can avoid the steep part of the hill."

"It's nice of you to help me, but I don't know why you are. It's plain you never, ever, really cared and all it took was a few minor incidents to make you hate me!" She could have bitten her tongue, but it was too late to take the words back.

"*A few incidents?* That's not what I'd call what happened

with us. But despite all that, I don't want you to have any more accidents while you're here for the wedding."

"Well if you can't forgive me for my *failings*, can you at least be civil through this weekend? We're no longer in each other's lives. You got what you wanted. And I'm okay with it," Abby stated, more firmly than she felt.

"All right, Abby. I'm sorry for what I said to Sam. I shouldn't have."

"Thanks," she said begrudgingly. She frowned and hobbled on, but the terrain was uneven and when she put her foot down on some uneven ground, pain seared through her hip and backside. "Owwwww!" she cried out and tears stung her eyes. She groaned for the pain in her backside, but also for the ache Jack brought to her heart.

"You *are* hurt! Damn it."

Almost in tears, she shrugged off his concern. "No. It's probably just a bruise, I'm sure. I'll be okay in a moment. I did twist my ankle, but it's not bad. And at Carly's wedding I have to be able to walk. But I think I'll be good to go."

"We'll get ice." He placed his arm around her. To be so close was almost more than she could bear—and she realized she still wanted him.

"Thanks, Jack," she said more calmly than she felt.

He gave her a sideways glance.

Abby raised her chin. "Are you comparing me to Monica?"

"Well, that's not what I was thinking at all, but I can tell you Monica would never get herself into this kind of trouble, in the first place. She would have looked before she walked."

"No, you're wrong, Jack. *Monica* wouldn't have bothered to walk at all. She would have sat tanning herself safely on the beach, and been about as exciting as a box of rocks. Still, she'll be fantastically pulled together, cool, and as always—*perfect* and elegant to look at. Monica's not much of an outdoors girl, is she?"

"No, not really, and she doesn't like to go on ski trips like you and I used to take. She's not into cold weather."

"I'll bet when you take her to a ski resort, she probably likes to sit in front of the fireplace, while you ski." Abby sighed and added wistfully, "I miss skiing."

A dark shadow passed over his face, but then he swooped Abby up in his arms, surprising her.

"Jack—"

"Your hobbling is getting to me."

"I'm sure I must be a mess."

He smiled down into her face and chuckled. "A bit."

"There's dirt on my clothes. I hope it's not rubbing off on you."

His brilliant green eyes, fringed with dark eyelashes, widened. For a second, warmth sizzled within. "Rubbing sounds a little suggestive?"

She cringed. "I didn't mean it like that."

His mouth turned downward. In a flash, he broke eye contact, though he continued to carry her.

She hung onto his shirt, which meant putting her hand on his chest. She was aware of his muscles rippling beneath her palm and that his hand was an inch away from her breast. His other arm cradled her backside.

An aching, need blossomed inside her. She could feel Jack's heart beating and was aware of wherever their bodies touched. When heat shot through her lower belly and her nipples tightened, she bit her lip, conscious of how the tips of her breasts nearly brushed his chest. Could he tell she was still attracted to him?

She hadn't been with anyone since Jack… Or before him. She wrinkled her brow in frustration. Her reaction to him perplexed her. None of the guys she'd dated affected her like he did, and she couldn't understand the power he had to unsettle her.

He carried her the rest of the way to the beach in silence.

She was such a fool. To him, she was the girl who always landed herself into trouble, or caused him trouble—which was the truth. Likely, he couldn't wait to get back to "safe Monica." Frowning at her thoughts, Abby lowered her lashes to make sure she didn't get eye contact with him.

When they neared the boat, resting in the mud on the shore, Jack strode into the picnic area with Abby still in his arms.

With a cool expression, Monica rose from her chair. She crossed her arms over her chest.

Sam strode in at the same time they did.

"Abby! I couldn't find you. What happened?" He spread out a blanket on the grass. "Here, let me help you."

Jack lowered Abby to the blanket. "She had a fall," he said in a flat tone.

Abby winced. "Ouch."

Jack narrowed his gaze on her. "Should we go back to the house? Do you need a doctor?"

Abby stretched out her leg, testing her sore foot. "No, I'll be okay."

Jack snorted in disbelief and dropped on his knees at her feet. "Let me see your foot."

She didn't want him touching her again or chance him noticing her attraction for him. Not that he would act on it, but Abby didn't want to humiliate herself in his presence.

Really…it was pathetic of her that she still had feelings for Jack.

"No, Jack, I'd rather you didn't," Abby said.

Jack ignored her request and removed her shoe and sock anyway. While Monica and Sam retrieved the picnic things from the boat, Jack reached in the cooler and made an icepack to drape around Abby's foot.

She watched as he gently held her foot in his hands for a moment. Big mistake. He looked up and met her intense gaze. Warmth sizzled through her.

Jack lay her foot on the blanket. "I hope that's better," he said gruffly.

Surprised by the terseness in his voice, she pointed to her backside. "If you must know, it hurts more here. I'm sure I'll have a big bruise. Something you can't help me with."

His lips turned into a half smile at her words, but he ignored her faux pas. Abby's cheeks heated. She was making a fool of herself.

Jack poured water from a bottle and wet a napkin. "Your face." He pointed to his right cheek and the tip of his nose. She took the offered napkin. As if he didn't want to be so close to her, he moved away on the blanket.

Abby wiped her face, and then rolled her eyes. "I guess I can't tell you to go to hell this time, Jack, especially since you've been so nice today. But I am glad you don't live around here anymore. Are you headed back to Florida soon?" She took a deep breath, and then blurted, "I think distance between us is better for me."

She bit her lip and frowned, but why lie to him? He had hurt her in the past—she had loved him—and he had dumped her. But here he was now, having the same old effect, making her feel warm all over—*and* he was being nice… How was she to survive the weekend?

"No, Abby, I'm actually not leaving after the wedding. I bought McAlister Construction. I'm bringing the company back into my family and I'll be living close by."

"*McAlister Construction!* Are you kidding me? Well, then I guess I can't tell you to go to hell. I work for the company—your new company. In the offices." She gulped. "Did you know?"

Jack shook his head.

The blood rushed to her face. "I guess you'll fire me now—and I have my condo mortgage to pay—jobs are scarce."

"Why would I do that, Abby?" he asked, penetrating her with his gaze. "Do you do a bad job?"

"No! Of course not. I'm always diligent at work."

"Then why would I fire you?" He raised a dark eyebrow.

"I thought perhaps you wouldn't want me around, or you wouldn't want to have me in your face, or you're afraid I'll do something else to wreck your life. To be honest, it will be hard for me to work there with you around. I don't know if I can do it. I may have to find another job..." Tears rushed to her eyes. "Damn it," she said, swiping the moisture away.

They'd had the coldest breakup on record, so she wasn't going to cry in front of him now. He had not even returned the several calls she'd made to him. Bitterness assailed her that he hadn't thought she was important enough to even reply. Afterwards, she hadn't lowered herself to call him again either. She had meant nothing.

Jack's brow furrowed, but he didn't get the chance to say anything because Monica and Sam walked over.

Monica nudged herself in between Abby and Jack on the blanket and began to chatter. "Jack, I told Sam that you bought McAlister Construction and he said Abby works for the company." Her gaze roved over Abby. "What a small world?"

Abby nodded. "Yeah, I guess so. Jack just told me he's acquired the company and will be relocating back to Ohio."

Monica pursed her lips. "Now this should be interesting."

Abby shrugged and said nothing to Monica's blunt statement because she had been shocked herself by this same turn of events.

While they ate a delicious gourmet lunch of various sandwiches and salads that the staff had prepared, and shared a few bottles of German beer, Abby contemplated the long weekend in front of them. Not only did she have to put up with him all weekend, but Jack was going to become her new boss, and Monica was soon to be his wife. *Terrible!*

Desolation sank into Abby's soul as she thought of Jack and Monica, married.

Wanting to hide how *pathetic* she was feeling about that, Abby tried to focus more on Sam during lunch and tried to be friendly. However, Sam misread her attempts to put him at ease and responded too eagerly, Abby cringed. Maybe being overly friendly with him wasn't a good idea, until she was sure she wanted to date him.

And seeing Jack had made her as unsure as hell.

Could this weekend get any worse?

* * *

After lunch, Jack and Sam carried the cooler to the boat to pack up for the return trip.

Jack lifted his end of the cooler onto the bow and didn't

have much to say to the man who might become Abby's boyfriend. In fact, his stomach rolled at the thought, and he didn't like the jealousy that ate at his gut. He'd met Sam years before through Abby's brother.

Sam narrowed his eyes on Jack, and then his gaze darted away. "I was surprised you bought the company, Jack. Since my stepfather owns Preston Construction, you'll be his newest competitor."

Jack shrugged. "I suppose so, but there's plenty of work to go around. So tell me, how is your stepfather?"

Sam raised his chin. "Ralph is doing great."

"I am glad. I hope he'll have no hard feelings about me taking over McAlister."

"If you've ever met my stepfather, you'd know he's the kindest man in the world," Sam said in a cool tone. "Ralph doesn't get mad—or try to get even. You can ask him how he feels about your acquisition when he arrives for the wedding. He won't mind your owning McAlister Construction as long as you run a clean business, without any shady tactics engineered to hurt his company."

Insulted at the dig, Jack clenched his hands. "Of course, I will run a clean operation."

Sam cocked his head. "I hope so as my stepfather's already had some sketchy dealings with Burns Construction. One dirty company in this area is enough."

"I'll remember that it is," Jack said frowning, not sure how to take Sam. He had been anticipating a conversation about Abby, not the business. However, he would watch his back with Burns...and the Prestons.

They retrieved more items to put on the boat. Then Jack went to help Monica pick up the rest of their picnic items. While she was bent over, he glanced over the top of her head and watched Abby as she limped in the direction of the boat with Sam by her side. Jack still reeled from being near her… Now, there was the disturbing fact that the woman who had betrayed him would be working for him.

"Perhaps Abby just didn't want to help us clean up after the picnic. What do you think? Maybe it was easier to pretend she was hurt than to do her share," Monica suggested.

Jack jerked his attention back and helped Monica pack things away in the basket.

"Monica—Abby *did* hurt herself."

"If you say so," she said in a voice that hinted otherwise.

Jack threw another glance toward Abby. He'd always been drawn to her like a magnet. Though she'd suggested he thought she was a mess in comparison to Monica, he had actually been thinking how adorable Abby looked with that dash of mud on her cheek and nose. For sure, she wasn't always pulled together like Monica, and nor was she boring…

Jack frowned as he watched Sam and Abby continue toward the boat. He was too far away to hear their conversation, but he noticed when Sam put his hand on Abby's waist, just above her shapely butt.

Jealousy ripped through Jack, and he didn't like the feeling one bit. He scooped up the picnic blanket.

Monica took two ends out of his hands and assisted him in folding it. "I've missed you so much, Jack, while you were away. I wish you'd let me visit."

"It was too dangerous for you, and too hot. You wouldn't have liked sweating. Your hair—"

"And with your decision to buy McAlister, we'll have to

move back to this cold climate now. You know how much I hate snow and freezing temperatures. And then to top it off, Abby will be working for you. She had to have set this up, Jack."

Jack shook his head in disbelief. "Monica, *no.* She says she's been working for the company for a while. She wouldn't have known anything about my struggle to acquire McAlister so this isn't any kind of plot."

In reality, he had never asked Monica to move with him to Ohio—at least not yet. And they had never even lived together. She wanted more, but he thought she might change her mind because of the cold weather. He actually hoped she'd decide to end this—whatever she thought *this* was.

Something—*some reason*—always held him back from making a commitment to her. Seeing Abby today reminded him why…

"Okay, Jack, but she hurt herself just as you happened to be around to help her, didn't she? Do you think that could have been deliberate or that she's faking it? A bit too coincidental, isn't it?"

Jack snorted and picked up the cooler. "You're saying it was some kind of ploy?"

"No, I wouldn't say that about Abby, as in that it was *deliberate.* I think she might have regrets and be pretty desperate seeing us together. You're a catch, for sure, Jack. She always wanted what she couldn't have and fought to get every man's attention when I was her roommate. It was her own fault she lost you. She shouldn't have slept with Vince or been so loose with other men. You were bound to find out eventually."

Pain assailed Jack—pain he'd thought he buried with

the past. "If I hadn't stopped by the apartment while she was gone," he said under his breath, "I would never have known."

"Do you think Carly likes Abby all that much? Maybe Abby somehow tricked her way into being in the wedding party too." Monica shook her head as if she couldn't believe this was happening.

Jack reared back. "Monica, Abby and Carly have always been the best of friends." Of all the things that he counted against Abby, questioning the sincerity of their friendship was not one.

He glanced up to see Sam loop his arm around Abby as they neared the boat.

Jack's mood blackened further and he clenched his jaw. Abby had cheated on him. He'd seen the evidence with his own eyes. As much as it had hurt him to break up with her, he wouldn't be played the fool the way his father had been.

Monica's lips curved. "Looks like Sam will get lucky tonight, Jack. So, just please, accept Abby for the way she is. She has that fresh appearance, but beneath it, she's not so innocent. She's just a passionate person who likes to satisfy her passions wherever she can."

Jack clenched his teeth. He knew intimately how passionate Abby was. Hell, it wasn't something he'd ever forget. And he'd been turned on today just carrying her in his arms. He also knew every delightful curve of her body that she would share with Sam and whomever else she wanted this weekend. He almost growled with frustration.

"Jack, did you see the way she kept leaning toward Sam, to give him a hint of her cleavage?"

"I did not," Jack retorted. He did notice the dip in Abby's shirt, but it revealed even less than Monica's. He narrowed his eyes on Monica. "I doubt Abby would say such things about you—even if they were true."

"I'm not trying to make you mad at Abby. Deep down, she is still my friend, even though she's angry with me. She knows she blew it with you. I'm just worried she'll take it out on me this weekend because we're together."

Jack gave Monica a pointed glance. "I haven't seen her angry with you at all. Abby would never do anything so mean."

Monica raised an eyebrow. "Has she talked to me or made an effort to be friendly since we've been here?"

"No, but if she hasn't, it is more about her past relationship with me, not because she holds anything against you."

"Well, she is angry at me. I can tell by the looks she's given me...behind your back."

"Abby…?" he asked, frowning again.

"I shouldn't say this, but she's that way—*sneaky.* You were once close to her, but you don't know how she really is."

"I suppose a person's character always shines through..."

Jack's stomach clenched as he watched Sam help Abby into the boat. It would be like a kick in the groin if she went to bed with Sam tonight. Jack wondered if he would ever recover from her. It was as if she owned a piece of his heart, no matter what she'd done to deserve the breakup.

"Jack?" He turned to see Monica's face harsh. "You've looked at her way too long. Will you show me I have nothing to worry about? I've missed you. You've been gone for so long... I need you."

Had she missed him? Or was this another attention-grabbing maneuver? She hadn't seemed to mind his other long trips out of town. Originally, he'd thought of their relationship as something more casual and that's what she said she wanted. He certainly hadn't wanted anything more. However lately, Monica had pushed for something more serious.

Monica threw her arms around his neck. "Jack," she whispered, "if you keep staring at Abby, I might have to insist you fire her."

His brow furrowed. "If I committed to you, you'd never have to worry about me being trustworthy, Monica. Abby could work at my company. She won't affect me at all. I'll never forget what she did to me."

Monica beamed a smile up at him. "Okay, then let's just get along with her this weekend, for my sake, because I want a pleasant weekend."

"For your sake, Monica." Jack understood her jealousy and squeezed her shoulders. Monica didn't deserve to be hurt this week just because he had lingering feelings for Abby. He nodded.

However, seeing Abby with someone else reminded him that he should be grateful to have a trustworthy woman like Monica. Steadfast and loyal—so what was wrong with him?

Jack picked up the cooler and together, he and Monica headed toward the boat.

"Jack, you know I like Fort Lauderdale. Why don't you sell the company or cancel the takeover? Then we wouldn't have to move here at all."

"I'll understand if you want to stay in Fort Lauderdale. It gets really cold here..."

As Jack neared the boat, he paused. Annoyance shot through him when Sam lifted Abby's leg to put her foot up on the back bench. Jack couldn't see Abby's face, but Sam smiled at her.

Jack barely heard Monica's next words.

"Guess I'll have to endure the cold, if we're moving here," she said, extending her arm around his waist. "You should really consider firing Abby though because I'll be uncomfortable with her working for you. You know that she's always going to think that I came between the two of you. She might want to get even with me. You don't know her at all, Jack..."

CHAPTER FOUR

Later that evening, Abby stepped into the ballroom for dinner. Music played and voices carried across the crowded room. She heard familiar laughter and turned to see Jack and Monica sitting at one of the dining tables near the entrance. Wanting to avoid them, Abby headed to the opposite side of the room.

When Sam strode toward her looking like he'd been watching for her, Abby quickly sat down at a nearly full table to avoid sitting with him—and from the disappointed flash in his eyes, he didn't miss it either. Sam reluctantly sat in a vacant chair at another table and continued to stare in her direction.

He'd expected to sit with her… Abby blew out a guilty breath. She had not meant to mislead Sam earlier. Unfortunately, on the excursion, she'd discovered that her feelings for Jack were still too strong to lead anyone else on, particularly Sam.

In addition, whatever Sam wanted to explore between them could not be explored with Jack in the vicinity—possibly watching. Abby inwardly groaned at her stupidity. Jack probably had not an ounce of interest in watching her, yet it still mattered to her what he thought. She was pathetic to let Jack do this to her! Jack, her *ex*, was marrying her *ex*-roommate.

She should have sat with Sam and tried to enjoy his company.

Mr. James Farrington had planned another lavish entertainment for his guests and several bands were lined up to play after dinner.

Abby took a trip to the restroom. When she returned, she realized she was standing only a few feet away from Monica.

Sadness and acceptance washed over Abby. Even if he couldn't be with her, she wanted Jack to be happy. She really couldn't blame Monica for wanting him. In addition, Jack wanted Monica. In frustration, Abby blew out a deep breath. She had to get over him, once and for all. Whatever that took.

Abby's shoulders stiffened as she was forced to acknowledge Monica's presence with a nod.

Monica edged closer as if she wanted to have a conversation. "Abby, I've talked to Jack about his attitude. He has assured me that he can get along with you for the weekend, even though he said it will be difficult."

Abby's mouth dropped open, then she snapped it shut, feeling as if she'd been insulted by Jack—and he wasn't even here. "*Difficult?* That's very big of Jack that he thinks he can get along with me for this weekend. I'll try not to be too *difficult*," she said with bitter sarcasm.

"We're to be engaged, you know."

"So you've said," Abby stated flatly. *So many times.*

"We're happy to be here to get ideas for our own wedding."

"I'm so *glad* for you, Monica," Abby muttered under her breath.

Missing Abby's sarcasm, Monica said, "I thought about

asking you to be my Maid of Honor."

Shock ran through Abby. "*Me?* I don't think so..."

Jack walked up to them.

"On your plans, I'm happy for you both," Abby said directly to him, while trying to keep the bitterness out of her voice. "And I'm sure you'll *both* be very happy, but I don't want any part of your wedding."

His face looked angry—and he had no reason to give her that look.

This is ridiculous.

Abby sighed. "I mean it, Jack. I want you to be happy. You can't make me angry anymore. Now if you'll excuse me—"

"Abby," Sam called out as he strode over to them.

Carly rushed up and clasped his arm. "Sam, would you please dance with Stella?"

She hauled him over to one of her female cousins, a shy-looking woman.

Then Trent arrived and extended his hand in invitation. "Monica, would you dance with me? You don't mind, do you, Jack? We'd all like to get to know your *future wife.*" Those words hung in the air.

"Go ahead," Jack muttered. However, it was Abby who Jack looked to after Monica and Trent walked away. "Having a good weekend?" he asked her, probably because some politeness was required.

"I guess so."

"Why aren't you dancing?"

"No one has asked me to dance—" She gasped and put her hand to her lips. "Oh no, Jack. I don't mean for you to... I wasn't fishing for a dance."

"How's your ankle?"

"It's okay. Thanks for your help and the ice." Abby smiled at him. "It was never really that bad."

"Monica said it was just a ploy."

Abby gaped. "She said that?"

Jack shrugged. "She's worried you might want me back."

"It's a needless worry. By the way, I told you before—and it's embarrassing—but here's where I really got bruised, my ankle, not so much." She put her hand on the back of her hip. "But I can still dance."

"Then why aren't you?"

"No one's asked me." She shrugged. "I even asked one of your cousins to dance, and he made a lame excuse that he had to go wash his car. Then I saw him two minutes later dancing with someone else. It's like I'm a pariah with most of the single men around here."

"I have no idea why," Jack said blandly, brushing at a piece of lint on his jacket sleeve. Then he gave her a pointed look. "By the way, is Sam your new boyfriend?"

Abby wrinkled her brow. She didn't want to tell Jack anything about her life. "Does it matter, Jack? Can we put *our* past behind us for Carly's sake and her wedding—and more so now, since I'm an employee at McAlister Construction? I need and like my job."

"I can be professional. And I won't take our past relationship failure out on you at work."

Abby sighed. "Thanks." They didn't speak for a moment. Finally, to make conversation, she raised her gaze to his. "I guess you'll be buying a house around here?"

"Yeah."

"That should be fun. Are you looking for the kind we always talked about?"

"Yeah, I'd like to buy an older two-story, one much smaller than this lavish estate, but something historical that I can renovate and grow into and add on to."

"And with some land?" she asked.

He nodded. "Yeah."

"Ah, I suppose you'll have horses, too? And you'll have all this with Monica?" She winced at an overwhelming ache in her heart as she remembered older dreams.

Jack shrugged. "I don't know. Monica doesn't like horses."

"Are you still mad at me about your car?"

"Damn, Abby, I was never mad at you about the car."

She flipped him a smile. "Yes you were. You're just being nice now."

"No," he said with a straight face. "I'm not."

"You were furious. And, yes, you are." She gave him a wry smile. "It's okay. It was stupid and I'm sorry I ran off the road and into a creek. Really I am. I know how much that made you hate me. I know it's old stuff between us and you have another life now, but I ruined your car on the anniversary of the first day we met."

"Abby, you had an anniversary for everything. First day we met, first day we kissed, first day that we—"

"That's enough." She blew out a deep breath. "I know you never cared as much about things like our special anniversaries, but they were important to me. I never told you, but the day I went off the road, I went to pick up champagne and your present. I'd painted you a watercolor and had it framed. It was ruined in the water."

"I didn't know."

Abby raised her eyes. "I shouldn't have used your car, but mine was in the shop. I just wanted to surprise you…

Really, I'm sorry. I always seemed to be doing something wrong."

"I suppose I did come across as angry afterwards. My laptop was in the car… There was client info I lost...and you could have been killed. That shook me up." He shrugged. "But I got over it, Abby…*really*. If I was upset, it was because you could have been hurt in that accident. And once I knew you were okay, yes, I did rant about the car, but I didn't stay mad afterwards."

"You were worried about me? But the car was your pride and joy."

"Insurance paid for most of the cost to replace it. I redid the week's worth of work that I'd lost on the laptop, so we can forget all that. We're both fine now. It's all water under the bridge, like us."

Those words stabbed at her heart. "Yes…water under the bridge," she said with a sigh. "Okay, Jack, well...have a nice evening."

She turned to walk away when a tall man with a comb-over hairstyle strode in her direction. The guy, probably in his early forties, looked a little creepy with pork chop sideburns that accentuated his long cold face. She'd seen him before, watching her, on the first night in the ballroom, but hadn't given him much thought after that.

She tensed. He was definitely heading her way.

Jack must have seen him, too, because he stepped up to her again and caught her arm. "I don't know who this guy is, but I don't think you want to dance with him, do you?"

She shuddered. "No, not at all."

"Since we're putting this all behind us, why don't we dance? And Trent seems to be keeping Monica occupied. We don't have to hate each other, Abby, even though a lot of hurtful things happened between us."

"*You've got that right*," she muttered, but she was grateful to be saved from the creepy guy.

He gave her a puzzled glance.

"And I'm willing to be an adult about it and let all that go," she said with a shaky smile.

"Then let's bury the hatchet. Let's dance."

He held out his elbow to her and they stepped onto the floor just as the song ended. When she turned to walk away, he stopped her by reaching for her arm.

"We'll still dance," he said.

When the next song began, her heart raced. "Gee, just our luck… After all those fast songs now they're playing a slow one." She wrinkled her nose at him. "Are you sure you want to dance this slow song with me?"

"I'm not worried about it. I can handle it if you can."

When he touched her hand and put his other hand on her waist, she inhaled his scent and liquid heat swept through her. She shivered. At one time, he had been her Jack, her lover, and she'd thought he'd also been her best friend…

"Are you cold?" he asked.

Heat rose on her cheeks and she shook her head. "No… Uh, it's been a long time since we've been this close."

His eyes glinted with a harsh look. "Any loves in your life—*or do you have a lot dangling on the line?*" he added dryly.

Abby's head jerked up. "*A lot?* No! There is no one, to be truthful." She blushed and dropped her gaze to his tie. Why had she just told him anything about her life? She hadn't planned to—he'd broken her heart. He didn't deserve any details on anything she did, other than about work…and only because he would be her boss.

"Is Sam just your latest conquest?" Jack asked again as they moved around the floor. She couldn't believe the jealousy in Jack's voice and was uncertain as to why.

"Sam wants to go out with me, but we're not dating. We've been friends for a long time… I'm not sure that I'm ready for anything…permanent."

"Yeah," Jack agreed in a biting tone, "why settle for one, when you can have many?"

"Many?" she asked, frowning. "Well that's not it at all..." She'd just never met another guy who affected her the way Jack did. "What about you? Is Monica the right woman for you? I'm just glad we found out that I wasn't, before we wasted both of our lives."

"Yeah, you weren't the one," he ground out. When she tried to jerk away, he tightened his grip on her waist and hand. "Don't leave…*please.*"

"Why not?"

"I don't know."

"You're with Monica now." They danced for a moment.

"Monica is a good person," he stated in a flat voice.

Abby glared up at him. "*Is she?* I really don't know that, Jack."

He narrowed his eyes. "How can you say such a thing about your friend? She talked about including you in our wedding, how even though we had dated she'd consider you for her Maid of Honor. Under the circumstances she thought you might not want to do it."

"Monica thought of me? Well, yeah, she's right. That wouldn't be appropriate at all. And to be truthful again—even though I shouldn't share with you how I feel—it would be asking too much of me to expect me to be in *your* wedding," she blurted. "And instead of being friendly with me… If you must know Monica—"

"So you're saying she was *mean* to you? She said you would probably cut her down."

"No! I'm not saying it was her fault that we weren't friends. It was mine with her. I always felt inferior… I thought she was judging me, and that I came up short. So Monica and I were never really close."

The song ended. He gave Abby a long, hard look before he glanced around the ballroom. "Ah, it looks like another one of my cousins has cornered Monica. Would you care to dance one more?"

"Okay...but darn, I can't believe it's another slow song. Are you okay with that?"

He nodded, his green eyes gleaming.

Although bitterness swept through her, Abby let him swing her around in his arms again.

Abby had always thought Monica was kind of a cold fish. There was something not right about her. Then Abby rolled her eyes at herself. What woman wouldn't feel that way about another woman who ended up with the love of her life?

After a few minutes, Jack swore under his breath. "I want to forgive you, Abby."

Abby couldn't believe her ears and gaped at him. "Forgive *me?*" she blurted. "If anything, I'm the *injured party* here."

His eyebrows drew together. "That's not the way I see it."

They stopped dancing.

Abby lifted her chin and boldly met his eyes. "How can you say that, Jack?"

"Because it's true."

"You couldn't wait to dump me for her. You didn't care what I went through. You were cruel and…and *heartless.*"

"But the choice was yours. You *chose* what you went through—"

Abby crossed her arms over her chest. "Oh, I guess I should have returned immediately from Switzerland. From the trip my family had planned for years?"

People turned and stared at them.

"Let's discuss this somewhere else." Jack pulled her by the hand into a nearby room and closed the door. He glared at her. "You didn't even know how far along you were. What kind of level-headed woman screws up something like that?"

"I guess you think I'm irresponsible. And you didn't want the baby. You told me so."

"I didn't say it that way?"

"Yes, you did! You said 'I don't want a baby.' You said the timing was bad. Admit that you were glad that I didn't have the baby! I was terrified—I went through all of that alone, Jack. I nearly died. And you didn't even call me."

"Nearly died?"

"You couldn't wait to rush off and get into a relationship with—"

Speak of the devil. The door opened and *Monica* stepped into the room.

With her hand on her hip, Monica surveyed them. "I heard you were in here. It looks like you and Abby are in a serious discussion. Is everything all right, Jack?"

Tears burned Abby's eyes. "The *discussion* is over. I'm leaving." She strode toward the door just as Sam popped into the room. Her stomach clenched.

"I've been looking for you, Abby. Would you like to dance?" Sam asked.

"Yeah, sure." Shaken from her conversation with Jack, Abby exhaled in relief and let Sam lead the way.

As they stepped onto the dance floor, Abby wondered why Jack's words hurt her so much…

* * *

Jack watched Abby leave the room with Sam. She didn't look back so he had no clarification of what the conversation they'd had was all about.

What the hell had she meant? Why was she trying to turn this all around on *him*? *He'd* been the one betrayed.

Even though she'd argued the breakup wasn't her fault, he disagreed. In addition, he hated the barbaric way he had wanted to shove Sam into a wall just for clasping Abby's hand.

Monica put her hand on Jack's jacket sleeve. "What did she say?"

Jack stiffened. "Nothing." He was still unsettled, conflicted, over the disagreement and about how good Abby had felt in his arms.

"Nothing? I don't believe it. I don't like what she's doing to you, Jack. I think she's trying to get close to you again. Can you understand that I don't like it? Now that you're even more successful as a multi-millionaire, she must want you back."

"Abby's not trying to get me back," he grumbled.

"She might be loyal for a while, but it wouldn't last." Monica crossed her arms over her chest. "She's like your mother, Jack. Women like that can't be changed."

He knew the truth of that statement more than most people. His own beautiful mother had repeatedly promised his father she'd change, and then she'd go back out and have another affair. His father had been weak and forgiving, and after a while, just turned a blind eye. Well he wasn't going to be taken in by someone like that.

Jack's stomach felt like it was filled with rocks. "Let's don't talk about Abby."

CHAPTER FIVE

After her unsettling discussion with Jack, Abby returned to the ballroom with Sam. Though her legs felt shaky, she danced to one song before saying, "I'm going to bed." She wanted to get away and mull over her conversation with Jack, which had made little sense.

A smile edged Sam's lips. He picked up her hand. "Is that an invitation to go with you? I have a long drive to my apartment, and *you* do have a room."

Abby gave him a sideways glance. "I thought Mr. Farrington gave every guest that didn't get a bedroom at the house, a room at the nearby hotel. That's not more than a quarter mile from the gates."

Sam cocked his head and his lips curved up at one corner. "So, he did. I do have a room there, but I'd still rather stay here at the house with you."

She tried to tug out of his grip, but he squeezed tighter.

She gritted her teeth. "I'm saying good night here, Sam. Have a nice evening."

Sam released her hand. "All right. I'll let you go, but only if you promise to play tennis with me in the morning."

Abby sighed. "Okay, tennis it is."

"Nine on the back veranda."

Not only did she have to worry about crushing Sam's

hopes, but the guy with the comb-over hair who she was certain had been about to ask her for a dance, crossed his arms over his chest and watched her as she strode across the ballroom to leave. The way he looked at her with lust in his eyes, sent an unpleasant shiver up her spine.

* * *

At nine a.m., with her tennis racket in hand, Abby met Sam on the back porch of the mansion.

"I hope you slept well?" he asked, stepping closer.

She stiffened and edged back. "Yes, I did."

"I hope you were dreaming of me." His smile sent an uneasy feeling through Abby.

Although she felt like retreating further, she stood her ground. She decided, after last night she had to tell Sam she didn't want to date him, even if her reason for that was because Jack was around. Sam and her dating, just wasn't going to work.

"You could have let me stay with you in your room last night," Sam drawled. He ran his fingers up her arm, sending a shudder through her.

Abby stepped back and realized her repulsion with Sam had nothing to do with Jack being here, but it came from deep within her. She didn't want Sam in the way he wanted her to. She had to tell him today, and clearly, that they could never be more than friends. *Sheesh.* And why was it, the more time she spent with Sam, the more he creeped her out? She just had to figure a way to let him down easy and not hurt him, and she decided that would be at the end of their tennis match.

She gripped her racquet and stepped off the porch. "Let's go to the courts."

As Abby strode in front of Sam down the steps that

descended the hill to the tennis area, Sam said to her back, "Really Abby, I was too tired to go to the hotel last night. I ended up sleeping on a sofa in the pool locker room. And I wasn't the only one crashing overnight after the party. The tall, balding guy staring at you last night crashed there, too. He said he had a hotel room, but he had drunk too much to drive. We weren't the only ones. I was lucky to find a place."

Abby frowned when she heard that even Sam had noticed that man watching her. She'd have to ask Carly who he was, but she really needed to deal with Sam right now. If Sam expected her to take pity on him because of where he spent the night, she was not taking the bait.

"Let's just play the game, Sam, okay?"

When they approached the courts, another couple was already having a match on one of the two courts, so they headed to the second. To Abby's chagrin, Jack and Monica were strolling in the same direction.

Abby muttered under her breath, "Can this morning get any worse?"

"Huh?" Sam asked.

Abby shook her head. "Never mind."

Monica looked pulled together in her designer tennis outfit, with a ruffled pink skirt, sleek hair, and perfect makeup. In comparison, Abby had applied minimal makeup, wore an orange t-shirt and faded blue jean shorts, and had pulled her long hair back in a ponytail.

Abby's gaze snapped to Jack who was as handsome as usual. Her heart raced, and she smiled, but realized it was an unfriendly gaze he pinned on her. In fact, the look was deadly, as if she'd done something wrong.

Her shoulders stiffening, Abby dropped her smile. He had no right to look at her like that, and why did he make her feel like she had to apologize? "We were just coming to play, too."

"*We?*" Jack cocked a dark eyebrow up at her and then threw a cold look toward Sam. "Enjoy your night?"

Abby jutted her chin in the air. *This was ridiculous! How dare Jack act as if he were jealous that she danced and played tennis with Sam—Jack was marrying someone else! Let him think what he wanted.*

"Yes, Jack," Abby answered through tight lips. "Sam and I are *enjoying* our time here this weekend."

Sam smiled at her as if she'd just given him the keys to her bedroom. Her stomach knotted, making her wish she hadn't said that. She ground her teeth together in frustration.

"Since there is only one court available, care for doubles, Jack?" Sam challenged. And so it began.

The first game, Jack and Monica won.

Monica had a cheesy grin on her face. "We're good, Abby," she said over the net. "You'll have to do better than that to beat us."

Whenever Abby looked Jack's way, he gave her a stony look. Puzzled, Abby was trying to read his expression when a ball whacked the side of her head.

Monica smiled like the Cheshire Cat. "Your turn to serve," she said in a sweet voice.

Abby gritted her teeth. After that, she pretended the ball was Monica's head. That really helped pick up Abby's game. She pummeled Monica with the balls every chance she got, and Monica usually missed. Abby and Sam won the tennis match, which left Monica pouting.

Jack strode up to the net, a steely gaze in his eyes and determination on his face. "Good game. A rematch?"

Mr. Farrington's English butler, Beasley, hurried down

the stairs to get to the courts. "Mr. Jack, Mr. Farrington says he needs to see you right away. Your cousins are already in the library."

"Excuse me," Jack said to Abby and Sam. "We'll have that game some other time."

Monica hurried behind Jack as he headed up the steps, leaving Abby alone with Sam.

Abby wondered what was going on because Jack rushed off as if it were something important.

Watching them go, Sam chuckled. "Jack didn't like us winning a game against him. He is so competitive," he said in a reflective and satisfied tone. "He didn't like that you were with me either. That is rich."

"Jack? Trust me, Sam. Jack doesn't care about me."

"You're right, Abby, he doesn't care about you at all. He went after your roommate."

Although the truth was a jab to her heart, Abby just shrugged her shoulder.

Sam gave her a knowing look. "He doesn't want you, but he doesn't want me to have you either."

Abby fiddled with her racket. "I have something to tell you, Sam..."

He looked away. "I have something to tell you, too. My stepfather needs to see me, so I have to leave today… I hope everything is all right with him. He's been acting strange," he said in a puzzled tone. He glanced back at Abby. "My stepfather and I will be back on Saturday for the wedding. Will you be here for me? I know where your room is. If we spend the night together, that will burn the shit out of Jack. You'd like that, wouldn't you?"

She reared back. "No!"

"You mean you don't want to get back at him, Abby,

for what he did to you with your own damned, stuck-up roommate?"

Abby winced. "Sam, this is what I wanted to tell you. I'm not going to date you, or do anything else with you. I've always thought of you as a friend. I can't help it, but I still do."

He gripped her arm, hurting her. "*A friend*, Abby? That's not how I want you to think of me. If you'll give me a chance—"

"No, Sam! And let go. I'm not going to change my mind."

"Damn. Jack gets everything. This has always been about Jack. Get over him. He's with *her* now."

Sam's face reddened. He took his racket and whacked it against the net, almost hitting her.

Abby gasped and stepped back. She had never seen Sam angry, but this did it for her. "I told you upfront that I didn't think it would work with us dating."

"There is no reason you shouldn't like me, except for *him*." He spit out the last word. "He dropped you for her, Abby. I'll be back on Saturday. By then you'll be sick of seeing them together, and stop being a loser."

Her cheeks burned.

Sam whirled and stalked off the tennis court.

* * *

After dinner, Jack stood talking with his cousin Trent in the ballroom, while Monica returned to their room to freshen her makeup.

When Abby walked into the room wearing a short, elegant blue dress, with a lacy overlay at the top, Jack couldn't keep his eyes off her. The dress hit a few inches above her knees and displayed her fabulous legs. Her hair was arranged in a pretty style and flowed down her back.

Jack couldn't deny the effect Abby had on him. He blew out a deep breath, realizing that with his attraction for her he might actually have a hard time working with her. If they were close...

"She's beautiful and you like her, don't you?"

Jack turned to Trent in horror. "What did you say?"

With a knowing look, Trent grinned. "Of course, I'm talking about Monica—not Abby. You're planning to marry Monica, aren't you?"

Jack shrugged. "That's what she's pushing for, but to be honest I haven't asked her yet." It was the furthest thing from his mind since he'd arrived. After seeing Abby again, he found his mind filled with thoughts of Abby and remembering what they had shared. The good times seemed to overshadow all that had gone wrong with them...

"After our meeting today, Grandpa told me he discovered that someone on the guest list might be behind the threatening call he received earlier. He said to tell you to keep an eye out. Last night someone was rifling around in his private office upstairs and it could be the same person."

Trent left to speak with other guests.

Monica entered the ballroom and linked her arm with Jack's. Together they walked across the room.

It was not lost on Jack that he couldn't remember the dress Monica was wearing this evening, while he had noticed Abby's and every curve her blue dress had emphasized.

Carly and one of her bridesmaids walked across the stage and Carly took the microphone. "We're instituting a few games."

After the girls stepped down, they drove the couples together in a line. "This is how it goes," Carly said as she pushed Abby next to Jack and Monica. "Boy, girl, boy, girl."

"But, Carly," Abby said in a helpless voice, "I don't have a partner."

Carly smiled. "I'll find someone for you."

"Too bad Sam left," Monica said with dry sarcasm. "He's the perfect match for you, Abby. What a great couple you two make."

Jack caught the conflicted look that passed over Abby's face. Maybe Abby wasn't into Sam as much as Monica alleged she was.

Grasping his elbow, Carly pulled Jack's cousin Chris over. Jack gave him a sharp, warning glance and Chris's shoulders drooped. "Looks like I'm wanted elsewhere. Sorry, Abby."

The tall guy with the comb-over stepped up to Abby. "I'll be glad to be your partner. How about it, sweetheart?"

This was the same guy who had approached Abby yesterday. Jack didn't know about his connection to Carly or Miles, but that wasn't unusual with the number of guests here this weekend. However, one thing was certain, he didn't like the way the guy eyed Abby as if she were a piece of candy.

Jack frowned as jealousy ripped through him again, but he realized he'd be jealous no matter who partnered with her. It hadn't been his feelings for her that broke them up.

Chris stepped up again. "On second thought, I *will* be Abby's partner."

"Okay," Abby agreed, obviously relieved.

Chris gave Jack a lopsided grin.

Jack gritted his teeth. He didn't like that Chris would be with Abby one bit, but perhaps Chris was better than this stranger.

Jack whispered to Chris. "Who is this guy?" Chris shrugged and shook his head. "Maybe a relative of Miles?"

Carly explained the rules of the game. With everyone lined up, man-woman, each person was to pass the orange to the next person in line, without using their hands.

The contest began to whoops of laughter as in every row there were funny incidents in passing the oranges, and even more hilarious was how close one had to get to successfully pass the orange.

The man with the comb-over found a partner and Carly pushed them in next to Monica. When he attempted to pass the orange to Monica, she gave him a dirty look. With a huff, she grabbed the orange from the man with her hand.

With a sly look, Monica thrust the orange under her chin. She turned to Jack, pretending she had not cheated. Then she rubbed her body against his, raising some catcalls from his cousins through the crowd as he grasped the orange under his chin.

Jack turned. The next person he had to pass the orange to was Abby. Once again, he was struck by her beauty and old memories returned. He frowned and knew he had to control himself—she was his employee now, as well as his ex.

Jack could tell Abby tried to keep her distance. He proceeded to get closer, trying to touch her as little as possible, too, but also to play the game and get it over with.

Jack chuckled. "Abby, you're making this impossible."

When he moved in closer, her breasts pressed into his jacket. He stared down at her cleavage, aghast. She was so close that he grew hard. Desire rode him like a horse. She had to feel what she did to him.

Abby gasped. "Jack!"

"You didn't feel that."

"Yes, I did!"

"That shouldn't have happened. You're too close."

He held her by the waist to move her hips a little away, but that threw her off balance. Abby's breasts smashed into his chest. Then she managed to grasp the orange under her chin. When she turned away, the lacy part of her bodice was tangled with buttons of his jacket.

She still held the orange under her chin. "Jack," she cried, clutching his forearms. "I'm stuck." He wrapped his arms around her. Electrical heat shot through him. To have her so near was like old times.

She dropped the orange.

Laughter erupted around them.

Chris chuckled. "The game is over. Our line lost."

His cousin Trent clapped him on the back. "Way to go, Jack. You might have lost, but you win, too. You and Abby—together again."

Ignoring his cousins, Jack gazed down at Abby. She was so lovely. Memories of all those times he had held her in his arms rose in his mind.

"At least I can enjoy the view," he whispered to her. "But let's see if we can fix this."

His Aunt Gertrude blasted out a cackle. "Monica, you'd better step aside. It looks like those two are hogtied forever."

Aunt Beatrice blurted, "No getting loose this time, Jack."

Jack couldn't even guess what Monica's face must look like after those comments from his aunts.

Jack took Abby aside and slipped his hands between them to release her dress. That only made things worse, as he practically had to cup her breasts with both hands just to try to untangle the dress from the buttons on his jacket. All the while, he had to gaze down into her lovely cleavage… Still hard, he found himself growing from hard to rigid.

"Jack!" Abby gasped, catching his attention. Her eyes flashed at him.

"You're only making this worse if you move."

"This is so embarrassing. Let's sashay into the hallway or something?"

Monica strode up to them. "Hallway? That won't be necessary. Let me help."

She grabbed Abby's shoulder, put her hand between Abby and Jack, and yanked. Abby's dress ripped, revealing even more of Abby's breasts over the top of her lacy bra.

Abby clutched the torn material.

"Monica!" Jack blasted. "We were handling it!"

"I had to rip your dress, Abby," Monica said through clenched teeth, "because you two looked like you needed some help, and he is *my* fiancé."

Abby blew out a deep breath and her shoulders drooped. "I should have realized this material could get caught on your buttons before we started the game… Jack, I'm sorry I'm always causing some sort of disaster."

She turned and hurried away. Instead of heading upstairs, where he thought she would go to change her clothes, Abby strode through the French doors to the patio.

"May I repeat, Monica—we are not engaged *yet*," Jack said in a steely voice. "And why don't you stop mentioning our engagement because we haven't made it official? I haven't said *yes* to *your* proposal."

Monica's mouth gaped open. Jack left her that way.

He couldn't let Abby go like this. Feelings for Abby roared through Jack like a raging waterfall. When he saw the balding man who had tried to dance with Abby move to follow her outside, Jack made a beeline for the door. He wanted to protect her and apologize to her for Monica's actions as well as his own.

CHAPTER SIX

In need of fresh air, and trembling all over, Abby strode out of the ballroom and fled across the patio, leaving the laughter and music behind. She took the steps that led down to the boathouse. When she reached the moonlit lake, she leaned on the railing and took a few deep breaths of the heavy woodsy scent that filled the humid night. Stars overhead were obscured by clouds and dark sky. A feeling of oppression filled the night, matching her mood perfectly.

The months she had spent shedding tears for Jack should have been enough, but now the pain overwhelmed her all over again. She swiped at the moisture on her cheeks. All this anguish for a man who had never loved her. She was an idiot.

She reminded herself that in the past, all he'd really shared with her was their hot sexual chemistry that had raged between them. She felt his desire tonight, and had already faced that, for Jack, sexual attraction was all he had ever felt for her. And at least he'd never lied to her because he had never, *ever*, told her that he loved her. The loving part had been all on her end. Accepting that, feeling the way she did now made her doubly an idiot.

There was a stillness to the night and even the crickets were silent now. A tear rolled down her cheek but then she realized something else was falling...

Raindrops formed widening rings on the surface of the water. She shielded her face. She should have gone to her room instead of coming down to the lake. Perhaps she should run back to the house now and slip up the back stairs. If anyone saw her, she could blame the rain for ruining her eye makeup.

"Abby!"

She whirled around. A familiar dark figure moved into the light.

"Jack?"

"I followed you."

"Obviously, but go back before you get soaked too." She clenched her teeth and leaned back against the railing. She didn't want him to see her with tears spilling over her cheeks—*for him*. He'd know he had caused her distress.

"Just a little rain. I wanted to make sure you were all right."

She jerked her arms across her chest. "I'm fine."

The rain fell harder and pounded her hair and skin and still she stood there, praying he'd leave her alone.

Jack took her arm. "Why are you standing out in the rain? Let's go inside before we're completely soaked."

They crossed the wharf to the cottage next to the boathouse. Jack pulled open the screen door and followed Abby inside the quaint, little house.

"Although there is security on the grounds, my Uncle James said there might be cause for concern with a big gathering here. So I'm not sure that it's safe for you to wander around alone on the estate at night."

"All right, I'll be more careful."

"Why did you come here, Abby? Why didn't you just go

to your room and change your dress and return to the party?"

Abby clicked on a small table lamp, thankful that the light was so low it barely illuminated the darkness.

She dropped down on the loveseat, shivering. "Because what happened with my dress was totally embarrassing. It wasn't about changing and going back," she said through chattering teeth. She looked at him and frowned. "And why are you here, being so nice? I'm surprised you're not angry at me for causing you more trouble."

"I don't care what happened up there or what anyone thinks. Here, you look cold." He tossed her a mohair throw from the back of the couch.

"Thanks." She pulled her feet up beneath her and covered herself, wanting to curl into a ball under its warmth. "I'm surprised you're not with Monica." Pride caused Abby to thrust up her chin, but she couldn't keep the bitterness out of her voice. "I guess you found your fairytale after all…but *with her*."

"You're the one who believes in fairytales—not me. I'm a realist, remember?"

"Yeah, you two proved me wrong, didn't you? I could never get you to believe we had anything special." She drew in a deep breath and added on a dry note, "And you were right. *We didn't*."

There was just enough light to see his face. She hoped he couldn't see hers clearly and realize that her face was wet from more than the rain. *Would he guess?*

"Mind if I sit?" he asked.

"Go ahead." She was surprised when he chose the loveseat too and sat down beside her. It unnerved her, having him sit so close when he belonged to another woman. She gave him a sideways glance.

"You sure Monica won't miss you?" she muttered.

"Well, one thing about Monica, you know she won't come out here in the rain. She'd mess up her hair or ruin her shoes…" He gave Abby a dry chuckle. "Unless she thought I would meet up with you."

"Jack! I'm not in competition with her for you!" Abby blurted out. "You made your choice between us. She's perfect. So pulled together and beautiful. I could never compete."

His eyebrows drew together. "Abby, are you kidding me? You're gorgeous. You were always beautiful to me. That was not the issue between us."

"But I'm not *perfect*, that's for sure. She's probably never broken your favorite trophy, or done anything like plowing your brand new car into a creek with your laptop in the trunk."

His lips curving slightly, Jack folded his arms over his chest and shook his head. "No, and I admit all that was a big thing to me at the time, but most of all I was just glad you were okay, Abby."

"The stream was only a few feet deep," she said with a negligent wave of her hand. She didn't want to talk about wrecking his car again, so she changed the subject. "Monica likes you a lot. She even followed you to Florida when you relocated. And she's rich, too. I could never compare, so it's good you found each other."

Jack narrowed his eyes. "Her dad's a dentist. She's far from rich."

"Well, she always acted like she was."

"I'm sure she's been pampered enough to seem like it."

"Really, it seemed more than that," Abby said with a

frown. "And you know she's going to have a problem with me working at your company."

Jack shook his head. "She'll try, but I won't let her."

"We'll see. She seems to have a knack for getting her way."

"She won't interfere with my business."

Then a crushing, painful thought occurred to Abby. Monica and Jack might one day decide to have children together.

"Whatever happened with us, Jack? We never even talked about it."

"There was no need. It was obvious. Everyone makes his or her own choices in life. You made yours..."

"Do you mean my choice to go off to Europe? You could have come for a week, but you were a workaholic. My family had planned the trip for years."

He blew out a disgusted breath. "No, I'm not talking about Europe, but what you *did* before you left with your family, more than anything!"

"Yes, it was my fault that I drove a wedge between us. I ruined your precious car, which meant more than us! That one is easy. I know you loved that car and your files were important—but I could never compare to Monica either."

His brow furrowed. "I'm not talking about the car, the laptop, or Monica," he grumbled.

"It doesn't matter anymore why we broke up," Abby blurted, deciding she wasn't going to be the one to mention the elephant in the room—her pregnancy. It wouldn't make a difference anyway. The subject was just too painful to discuss, in addition to the fact that he'd deserted her in her time of need. She had the feeling the pregnancy had been *the* last straw, the final issue she'd piled on him—one he couldn't endure.

She winced. "It's okay Jack," she said more calmly. "We really don't need to talk about it. As you said, it's all water under the bridge with us. I just have to remember that. And I love you enough that I want you to be happy. I really do."

His face turned harsh. "When I first saw you this weekend," he said softly, "I was prepared to hate you."

"Why would you hate me? I may have done a few stupid things, but nothing to make you hate me!"

"For what you did to me—what you still do to me. Why do you bother to say you love me?"

"Because I still do, Jack. My misfortune."

He hesitated. "Seeing you again makes me realize that marrying Monica would be the biggest mistake of my life. Perhaps this is why." He reached out and stroked his finger down Abby's cheek. He traced her eyes, her nose, and her lips. "This feels like old times, Abby. Your skin, your mouth…"

Ignited by his touch, desire sizzled to her core.

He leaned in and brought his mouth closer. Then he pulled back, his green eyes flashing. "If you really loved me, Abby, you sure had a strange way of showing it."

"By going on a chance-of-a-lifetime trip, which my family had planned for years...?" She couldn't say *and the baby*. It was too painful, so she changed the subject. "How did you end up with Monica, Jack? Why *Monica*?"

He groaned. "Because of you… She doesn't make me feel what you do—out of control. I never want to lose control again. But that doesn't mean you still don't tempt me…" He put his hand on the back of Abby's nape and drew her to him. "I want to kiss you again, before I make any commitment to Monica, before you share it with Sam and everyone else."

"Share! What—?"

He ground his mouth down on Abby's lips and silenced her words. At first, she resisted his almost angry kiss, but then she melted into his embrace and looped her arms around his neck. He softened his kiss.

All thoughts gone, she didn't protest when his hand cupped her breasts, nor when he lowered her bra straps.

She dug her fingers into his hair. With the tear in the front of her dress, it was easy for his tongue to slide down her bare skin. He tugged her dress down to her waist. Her bra that hooked in front, he unhooked with ease. Cupping her bared breasts, he lowered his mouth and latched onto her nipple, sending shock waves through her.

Although heat flooded to her lower regions, she grabbed his arms. *This couldn't be happening.* "Jack! You're undressing me."

"Damn, Abby? I want to touch you—everywhere." Jack brought his mouth back to hers. He slid his hand under her dress and his fingers into her panties.

At the sensations he evoked in her, she moaned against his lips. It had been so long. She wanted him against all reason.

He jerked away. "You're still wanting it, aren't you? When I'm with you, even I forget what you've done."

Feeling mortified and breathing heavily, she pulled up her dress to cover herself, disbelieving what she'd just nearly let happen.

"What else have I done to you, Jack?" Abby asked bitterly. "Why don't you tell me just how badly I've been to you?"

"You got pregnant."

Anger sizzled in Abby. So her pregnancy *had* been the final blow to any feelings he'd had for her. "Last time I heard it takes *two*."

"You admitted that you missed your pills for several days."

"I did. I'm sorry about that. I misplaced them, but I didn't expect the repercussions to come so easily."

"You should have. But in the end, it's easy to see how well that turned out."

Abby jerked up her chin. "The baby...in all ways...was my fault. I was responsible for everything that happened with the pregnancy—"

"And you didn't even know if the baby was mine."

"The baby was yours! How can you suggest anything else?"

"You can't be sure. You knew, after my mother's behavior, that the one thing I couldn't tolerate was a cheater. You're as easy as she was."

"*Easy?*" Hurt roared through her. Abby reached out to slap his face, but he caught her hand. "I can't believe you said that to me. I was always loyal to you, Jack. I never cheated." She jumped to her feet. "Who do you think I am? You don't even know me."

Jack rose beside her. "Last night, I saw Sam outside your bedroom door, Abby. He acted like he just came out of your room. Why deny it?"

"If he was there, it was to test your ego, Jack! Sam probably did that so you'd think he'd been with me. He wasn't in my room. I have no idea why he was outside my door! And even if he was with me, why should you care? You're with Monica."

"What about in the past? The things in your bedroom

told another story, Abby."

She gaped at him, stunned. "What things? What are you talking about?"

With his hands on his hips, he glared at her. "Who the hell was the father of your child, Abby? Or would that just be a good guess on your part? You can lie all you want. I had the proof that you cheated on me."

"Jack, what proof?" Abby whispered. "What are you saying?"

"You didn't think I'd find out, did you? Monica tried to cover for you, being the good friend that she was. When I brought something over to your apartment for you while you were away in Europe, I saw things that revealed your true character, Abby. You could have at least tried to hide that you had someone else on the side—but then you rushed off to Europe. You weren't expecting me to show up at your apartment. Did I work too hard to build a future for us? Did I not spend enough time with you to make sure you were satisfied?"

Her stomach knotted. "I don't know what you're talking about."

With his breathing coming harder, Jack blasted, "It's pointless to lie. I had more proof—your sexy pictures with him posted on your social media page." Jack clenched his hands. "You were screwing Vince Michaels and most likely others."

She gaped at him, speechless.

"And, yes, I was jealous as hell, Abby, and I still am insanely jealous when it comes to you. If you're getting the cold shoulder this weekend from my cousins, it's because I told them—on the threat of death—to stay away from you."

Jack whirled and strode out of the cottage. The screen

door closed behind him with a resounding whack. She heard his footsteps on the dock as he strode away.

Abby gasped and slumped back on the loveseat. She was more confused than ever about what had happened to cause their breakup. However, a few things were coming into focus. No wonder Jack had broken up with her. Apparently, he'd seen something at her apartment that had made him think she was seeing someone else.

At the time, those faked pictures had mysteriously appeared on her social page. She had no clue that Jack had seen them, and they were very suggestive with her wearing a black negligee. They were obviously fake photos because the event had never happened, but Jack wouldn't have known that. The pictures had not been there for more than a day before she'd taken them down and changed her password! She had assumed Vince was the culprit.

Abby wrapped her arms around herself and headed for the house, shaking with adrenaline. Everything was becoming clearer as to why Jack had suddenly broken off with her.

The rain had stopped. As she walked up the steps, following the faint lights along the walkway, she saw a dark shadowy figure cut across the lawn in front of her. Abby picked up her pace and hurried toward the house. She didn't want to speak to anyone after all these revelations with Jack. She hoped it wasn't the man who seemed to be stalking her.

CHAPTER SEVEN

Friday morning, birds chirped outside the mansion. Colorful roses and flowers blew in the gentle, fragrant breeze as Abby stepped out on the back porch. The stormy weather of yesterday had cleared and promised that Saturday would be beautiful for Carly's wedding. The activities for the day had not yet begun.

Abby's stomach was in knots after the bomb Jack had dropped on her last night—he thought she'd cheated. Of course, she'd had trouble sleeping.

As soon as she saw Carly, Abby clutched her friend's elbow. "I need to talk to you privately. It's important. It's about Jack and me."

Carly's worried glance took in Abby's distress. "Okay, but let's get coffee."

At the outdoor station, they grabbed a cup and went to a wrought-iron table on the stone patio where they could sit in seclusion.

Abby stirred the cream in her coffee, still in shock from what Jack revealed. "You won't believe this. For some reason Jack thinks that back when we were together, I was also sleeping with Vince Michaels behind his back."

"Wow! Where'd he get that crazy idea?"

Disbelief still reeling inside her, Abby shook her head.

"Remember how I told you I'd been hacked on one of my social media sites and there were some pictures of me with Vince Michaels posted, looking like we were together and I was wearing a negligee?"

Carly's eyebrows drew together. "Yeah..."

"I just found out last night that Jack saw them." A cold knot formed in Abby's stomach. "Then he dropped this bomb on me that he'd brought something over to my apartment when I was in Europe and that he found *proof* that I was cheating on him."

"Jack was at your apartment while you were away?"

"Yeah, and I've been racking my brain for an answer as to what he saw. I always thought he broke up because I wrecked his car and something else..."

Guilt crept over Abby. She'd not even told her best friend about the pregnancy. When Jack had broken up with her, she had not wanted to say anything to taint Carly's feelings for Jack. Then the pregnancy...had not lasted. After that, Abby didn't mention it because she wanted to forget.

"What are you thinking about that has you so sad?"

Wincing, Abby shook her head. "Nothing, just all that 'water under the bridge stuff' with Jack."

"I just can't believe that Jack thought you were cheating on him," Carly said.

Abby brushed a strand of hair from her forehead and blew out a deep breath. "I know."

"What did he find?"

"I don't know, but it happened while I was in Europe."

"Was Monica there?"

"Yeah, he said she let him into our apartment and my room. I guess he was so attracted to her that he just wanted an excuse to break up with me—"

"Abby! I don't believe that." Carly leaned across the table. "That man was in love with you! Don't be so gullible. Think back. What could have happened to change things between you and Jack?"

Abby sighed. "Besides wrecking his new car and destroying his laptop? How much more would it take?" She didn't add about the pregnancy, which she knew would top the list as he'd repeatedly told her he didn't want children.

"Abby...what about Monica? Had you considered she might have set you up?"

"Monica? I can't believe she would have anything to do with those social media photos. Why would she lie and tell Jack I was seeing Vince? She was the one seeing Vince, along with a few other men..."

"She must have wanted Jack. Wise up, Abby. I don't put anything past Monica. And she must have planted not only the pictures, but something to make it look like you were cheating because Jack wouldn't just have taken her word for it."

Abby sank back into her chair. "Could Monica be that bad? Maybe...but if I told Jack what I suspect, would he believe me over her? I can't believe anyone would do something like that intentionally."

"I do! I think she's ruthless if she wants something. And I never liked her one bit. You should have seen the nasty looks she's given you since you've been here."

Biting her lip, Abby clasped her coffee mug in her hands and reflected for a moment. "Maybe… Slowly things began to change with Jack and me, after Monica moved into the apartment. She said he always watched her, and she asked me how I could stand that. I never saw anything, but I was so stupid—I believed her."

"You were always too insecure about Jack for your own good."

Abby nodded. "And I can't believe that *I* believed her without even confronting him. I was just so heartbroken and thought that he wanted to be with Monica." With hot tears stinging her eyes, Abby turned to Carly. "I wonder if she also told him horrible things about *me* behind my back?"

"I wouldn't put anything past her. She was going after Jack."

Abby's stomach swirled in knots. "How could I have been so stupid? It must have been Monica who faked those photos of me with Vince. I had suspected Vince, and confronted him, but of course he denied it with a laugh—the snake that he is. And the photos were spliced from several parties we'd attended, but he must have known what Monica did."

"And if Monica was the one to do this to you, Abby, she would have made sure Jack saw them."

"If so, it's scary the lengths she went to, to break us up."

"Jack is extremely handsome and on a path to success. Any woman would want him, and she steamrolled over you to get to him. I think she must have been trying to drive a wedge between you two from the beginning with all her talk about him watching her, when he probably wasn't at all."

Misery washed over Abby. "It worked. I didn't even put up a fight."

Carly crossed her arms over her chest. "So, if we're right, both you and Jack might have fallen for her tricks."

Blinking back hot tears that stung her eyes, Abby slumped back in the chair. "Yeah, but now, it's too late. He's in love with her. They're going to be married."

"I haven't seen any demonstration of love between them, and I can tell you that no one in the family likes her—and we *don't* want Jack to marry her. So what are you going to do?" Carly asked.

"Nothing. What can I do? We're only speculating that Monica did something, and if I told Jack outright what I suspect, he'd think it was sour grapes. I would just look like the liar he thinks I am. He'd never believe me."

"You give yourself too little credit. Jack was in love with you." Carly leaned over the table. "I have a confession to make. That's why I didn't tell you before you got here that he was coming this weekend. I was afraid you wouldn't come until the wedding. I knew if you two had time together, you might see you were meant for each other."

Abby clamped her arms over her chest and shook her head. "No. Even when we were together, before Monica, Jack never said he loved me. And if he did have some feelings for me back then, and even if she did something to break us up, Jack loves Monica now. Not me."

"So you're just going to do *nothing*?" Carly slumped back in her chair in disbelief.

"Yes, because he loves her, not me! And what if we're wrong? What if Vince did those pictures on his own and Monica had nothing to do with Jack and me breaking up?"

"Who besides Monica would have wanted to fake pictures of you with Vince? Do you think Vince would go to all that trouble just because you wouldn't sleep with him? You have to find out if she planted something at the apartment to make Jack think you cheated. You can't just let her get away with all of this if she did this to you and Jack, right?"

Abby clenched her fists. "No, I suppose I can't. But I

need to find out, not for me—but for one reason only—for Jack. He's the one who will be stuck with Monica for life, and he needs to know what he's marrying. And if he hates me for clarifying that—well, he hates me." She shook her head in frustration. "But what can I do to prove it? That is the question."

The two women put their heads together and made a desperate plan to confirm their suspicions and interfere in Jack's life.

* * *

Later in the day, Abby and Carly passed by Jack and Monica who were on their way to the docks to go for a boat ride.

Monica was friendly enough and even complimented Abby, but when Jack saw them he had a pissed-off look on his face. His expression almost made Abby want to cancel her plan with Carly for that evening.

After they walked on by, Carly asked. "Are we still on for tonight?"

Abby sighed. "Yeah, I guess so, but after tonight I'm definitely going to be looking for another job."

Their plan had to take place that night as the wedding and reception were tomorrow, then everyone would head for home on Sunday.

That evening, for the casual affair, Abby wore a blue-and-white sundress with high-heeled strappy sandals.

After dinner, Carly strode up on stage in the ballroom and took the microphone. "It's Karaoke night. We're going to have a contest. I hope some of you will come up and sing."

"Should we sing love songs, Carly, for the bride?" Chris asked from his place at one of the dinner tables.

There was some laughter and commotion in the crowd and some further making fun of love songs and their titles. Then a deejay proceeded to take requests.

Abby had purposely sat at the table next to Jack and Monica. While they talked, Monica laid her hand on Jack's arm. Abby tensed and then was disgusted with herself. Why couldn't she just accept the fact that they were together? But then what about their searing kiss the night before?

"Let's do a song, Jack," Monica said.

"Monica," he grumbled, obviously still in the same dark mood as yesterday. "I don't want to."

Monica placed her hand on her heart. "Oh, but you will—*for me*, won't you?" She flicked a snide glance toward Abby.

"Monica, you can't sing," he pointed out.

Monica gasped and clenched her wine glass tightly. "Why, Jack, you can't be serious? Of course, I can sing. I sing to you all the time. Are you saying you don't like my singing?"

"Monica, no..." He shook his head and didn't say anything more.

"Well," she huffed. "I'll do a song and show you that everyone else loves my singing." She strode onto the stage.

Monica sang an off-key version of *Somewhere Over the Rainbow*. When she screeched the high notes, everyone laughed. Monica frowned. "The music was in the wrong key for me. I'll sing something else."

That's when the deejay stepped up and took the mike from her. "That's great, darlin', but we have more folks who want to sing. We need to call up more contestants."

Embarrassed, Monica shoved her nose in the air, stalked off stage, and right out of the ballroom.

A few more singers graced the stage. Many were good and some were not so good, however, everyone clapped for them because it was all in fun.

Alex Drake, the handsome actor and blond cousin of Jack's, strode onto the stage with his guitar. When he sang, Abby was amazed and so was the crowd, judging by the applause. He gave a cheeky bow. Several of his cousins sent balled-up paper napkins flying at him.

"Unfair, Alex," Trent said, and they all laughed.

Alex threw them a dazzling smile before he exited the stage. No one stood a chance against such a pro.

Carly stepped up to the microphone. "I'm putting out a call for Team Jack and Abby."

Abby's eyes widened. "What the…?" she grumbled, gritting her teeth. That wasn't in their plans! So her dearest friend had found another opportunity to throw them together.

Abby glanced toward Jack and caught him staring at her. With his arms crossed over his chest, he stilled looked pissed at her from yesterday. With what she'd planned with Carly, Abby's spirits sank to her toes, while her nerves stretched tighter.

She and Jack shook their heads at each other, then turned back to Carly and simultaneously declined.

"Come on, Jack and Abby," Carly begged into the microphone. "Would you deny a bride her one request, and the real gift she wants from you two for her wedding? All I'm asking is for you to sing your two songs from back in high school. When Abby and I were freshmen, and you, Jack, were the Big Man on Campus, and a senior. Can't I talk you into singing?"

Jack didn't say a word, while Abby's shoulders tensed.

"Come on, deejay," Carly said. "Why don't you play a bit of their songs to motivate them? Here are the titles. As I remember it, these two won the high school singing competition that year."

As the music played, heat rushed to Abby's cheeks. Days ago, she should have realized no good could come of being so close to Jack. She should have gone home, missed these embarrassing events, and returned in time for the wedding. This was like being tortured. She stood, determined that she was going to forget the plan she and Carly had made for that night and go to her room.

Before she could make a hasty retreat from the ballroom, Jack strode toward her. He reached for her arm, sending a shiver though her. His face softened. "Abby, I can do this, if you can. *For Carly.*"

Abby nodded, still unsure, but she said, "All right, for Carly."

Once they stepped onto the stage, the deejay restarted the music.

During the intro music, Monica reentered the ballroom. Furious, she clenched her hands on her hips. If looks could kill…

"I'm sure we're a little rusty," Abby quipped as she took one of the microphones.

Abby did her best not to look into Jack's eyes, until she sang a line about heartbreak during the second song, where every word punched at her soul. Her eyes burned. She couldn't stop herself from turning to Jack. She took in his strong body…from his long legs, up to his shirt that emphasized his muscular chest. She snapped her gaze to his face and read the same bleakness in his eyes that was probably reflected in her own.

When the song ended, she and Jack stood staring at each other. Her heart lurched. If only she could get the chance to tell him that she thought he'd been duped about her, and how worried she was about his future with Monica.

Carly, who'd always been a ham on stage, but who was also tone deaf and couldn't sing, took the microphone, breaking the moment between Jack and Abby.

Abby sighed and returned to her table, and Jack to his.

More people sang, and at the end of the competition, two of Carly's bridesmaids collected the votes and tallied them.

Once again, Carly strode up on stage and took the microphone. "The top winners are first place, Alex, second place, Abby and Jack."

From his table, Alex informed them he was bowing out of the competition.

Jack and Abby moved into first place and good-naturedly accepted a couple of gag gifts, before stepping off the stage.

Chris cornered Jack and congratulated him, patting him on the back.

Monica stepped next to Abby and hissed, "No, matter how much you try to get Jack back, it won't work."

Abby held up a stopping hand. "I'm not here to have a catfight with you about Jack, but we need to talk. Can we go somewhere private?"

"I have nothing to say to you," Monica snapped.

Abby grabbed her jacket. She had to see this thing through and now was her chance. "Well, I have a few things to say to you, unless you want me to say them in front of Jack."

Reluctantly Monica followed Abby onto the moonlit

patio, where they could have a private conversation.

"I don't know what you're trying to do, Abby, but Jack loves me. He even wanted me when he was dating you."

Abby's stomach clenched at just how uncertain she felt. Could she be all wrong?

Monica jabbed her finger near Abby's face. "So all your attempts to throw yourself at him— your boobs in his face or your ass—it is not going to work. You'd be wise to take up with Sam."

"I'm not dating Sam."

Monica returned a cynical face. "Well *he* seems to like you, so take what you can get."

"I like Sam as a friend."

"I don't care who you like or how—just stay away from Jack."

Controlling her anger, Abby stepped closer to Monica. "How did you get Jack to believe I was seeing that guy you dated, Vince Michaels, Monica?"

Monica's eyes gleamed. "Maybe I thought you were seeing him, too, Abby," she said in a lying, tormenting voice. "I saw pictures on your social media. You were wearing a little black negligee that showed just about everything you have. Vince's arm was around you—"

"I was not seeing him and you know it!" Abby balled her fists. "You're the one who faked those photos. You put my head on someone else's body."

Monica didn't deny it and let out a dry chuckle of agreement. "Oh, Jack was really upset when he saw those pictures, Abby," she mocked. "And it didn't help your innocence when Jack found Vince's underwear lying on top of your hamper, a few male items like shaving cream and razors in your bathroom, and a jacket hanging in your closet... It certainly looked incriminating to Jack."

"That sleazy Vince was never in my room and you know it. Vince was your occasional *friend with benefits*, not mine."

Monica raised her chin. "Well, Jack seems to think Vince was in your room and that you were sleeping with him. As a matter of fact there were several packages of condoms lying on your nightstand."

Abby trembled, but she swallowed her anger. "You were the one who dated Vince. So how did Vince's things get into my room? You had to put them there. How could you have done that to me?"

Monica didn't implicate herself, but only shrugged. "Too bad for you, Abby, because Jack thinks Vince had been in your bedroom—*with you.* That reminded him so much of what his mother did to his father. And now Jack thinks you're a liar and a cheater, just like she was—"

"You did that to me! And I'm not a liar! You liked Vince because he was rich, but he only wanted you for occasional sex. I'm now sure you're the one who hacked into my social media pages and posted those fake photos of me with Vince, just to ruin me with Jack. You must have shown them to him."

Monica snorted. "Who cares, Abby? All that happened two years ago. Jack and I are going to be married now. And you, my dear, sweet ex-roommate, are out of the picture. So if I were you, I would look elsewhere for a job because when Jack and I are married..." She shook her finger at Abby. "I'll make sure you're fired."

Abby clenched her hands and stood her ground. "Jack already said if you two get married that he won't fire me." She didn't feel confident at all that it would still be the case after her encounter with Jack last night, but she wasn't going to let Monica know that. Matter of fact, she would probably be fired on Monday—if she didn't quit.

"He would fire you if there was a reason." Monica pushed her face closer to Abby. "Let's just say that there might be a little slip-up in your job performance at the company."

So close to shoving Monica out of her face, Abby worked to regain her composure. She fisted her hands and controlled her emotions. "So what kind of trick are you going to pull now to get me fired?" she asked through gritted teeth.

Monica laughed. "Anything I want to do. Jack was furious when he saw those pictures of Vince. He turned quite cold. Oh, Abby, you really, really hurt Jack so much. I had to make it up to him. It took a while before he would even date me."

Abby had remembered how cold Jack had been over the telephone on their last call.

"I didn't cheat on Jack. And you set me up. You used to tell me bad things about Jack, how he used to come on to you behind my back or when I wasn't around. Meanwhile, you were schmoozing to steal my boyfriend by any means, and you used his weakness because of his mother. I trusted you! I thought you were a good person, and that I should step aside because he really wanted you—*not me*."

Monica only lifted her shoulder in a shrug.

Angry now, Abby clamped her hands to her waist and jutted her face toward Monica. "You need to tell Jack the truth, Monica. You need to tell him that you set all this up with Vince. That this was all a fabrication."

"Are you kidding me? No way."

Taking in Monica's polished but cold appearance, Abby realized there had always been something devious about this woman. Monica's attitude had consistently been that she was above everyone else and deserved more—by any means. Abby had seen the horrible way Monica had treated her ex-friends.

Monica laughed and swung her perfect hair with a shake of her head. "It doesn't matter now. It's the past. Get over it. Jack is mine, and he'd never believe you."

Abby flinched at the truth of that verbal blow, which hit like a kick to the stomach. Why should Jack take Abby's words over Monica's when he'd seen what he must have thought was cold hard evidence that she had cheated on him?

Monica's lips curved in a smirk and she just couldn't leave it there. "Abby, good luck with, Sam. Don't be too sad. He seems to like you. And forget about being my Maid of Honor. I only wanted to rub in your face that Jack will soon be *my* husband. I thought I might enjoy seeing poor, pitiful Abby, so unhappy, and in the ugliest bridesmaid gown I could find. *Now*," she said, in a threatening tone, "I don't want you anywhere near Jack, and that includes on the job or in my wedding party."

Monica turned on her heel and headed toward the ballroom.

* * *

An hour later, Abby met Carly backstage in the sound equipment room of the mansion.

Abby held out her palm with her cell phone. "We were right. Monica might say Jack won't believe me, but here's my proof to convince him. My conversation with Monica, fully recorded. There's even more here than I bargained for."

Carly smiled and took the cell phone. "Good girl."

Anger sizzled inside Abby. "I still can't believe what she did to Jack and me, and she won't tell him the truth."

"Then she left us with no choice."

"Yeah."

Abby followed Carly to the entertainment equipment and plugged the cell phone in the docking station.

Carly placed her finger on the play button. "Are you ready?"

Abby drew in a deep breath and nodded. "As ready as I'll ever be."

"Okay. Here goes."

While the recording started, they took a spot close to where Jack and Monica sat at a table. They listened as Abby's conversation with Monica played, blasting on the speakers for all to hear.

As the conversation played in the ballroom, all chatting stopped and the guests listened attentively.

Abby gazed back toward Jack. She saw his face harden into an angry mask again, as he listened. Her spirits sank. He was going to hate her for this.

She clutched Carly's arm. "Oh my! I shouldn't have done it. Have I done something awful to him again?"

Carly's pale face didn't reassure Abby at all.

After the recording ended, Monica's face reddened. She grasped Jack's arm. "Jack, it's a joke! I only said those things because Abby made these *ridiculous accusations* against me. She edited it to say what she wanted you to hear, too. She's nothing but a liar, trying to make me look bad."

Her heart pounding in her throat, Abby strode to them. "Jack, you need to know I didn't change a word she said. And I never cheated on you. I wasn't seeing Vince or anyone else. It was all lies made up by Monica to tear us apart."

"Whose word are you going to take, Jack?" Monica turned and gave Abby a deadly stare. "Thanks for trying to destroy my relationship with Jack. *We* are happy. *We* are in love. So now you have publicly humiliated him in front of his family and friends. And, for recording me without my permission, you can expect to hear from my father's attorney."

Heat rose on Abby's cheeks. Uncertainty hit her as she glanced around the room and realized that, to the other guests, this might seem like a prank. It might even have backfired and she could come out of this looking pretty bad—not Monica.

Stone-faced, Jack just stood there as he tried to control his anger.

Abby's stomach tightened into knots. She should have given the recording to Jack quietly. Once again, she had done something to harm him. No matter what he thought of the recording, or how he'd connected with her ex-roommate in the beginning, she had humiliated him and the woman he loved, and she'd done it in front of his family. Now, this could go badly and he would hate her even more.

With her throat and heart aching with despair, Abby turned and fled through the patio doors.

CHAPTER EIGHT

Jack watched Abby's retreating back as she rushed from the ballroom and into the night. Then he turned his anger full force on Monica. "You lied! You misled me!"

Monica clamped her hands on her hips. "Don't believe Abby, Jack! Didn't I tell you she would get even with me because we're a couple? I was joking with her because she's ridiculous—and a liar. And it's *me* you love."

"You are the liar, Monica. It's over for us." He'd had enough. "Now pack your bags. You're going back to Florida as soon as possible. With what you did, I'm sure Carly doesn't want you at her wedding either. I'm calling my assistant to arrange your flight and a cab to pick you up in twenty minutes."

He pulled out his cell phone.

"But, Jack—"

"We're through, Monica. If it's any consolation, I wanted to break it off with you anyway. After coming here, I began to realize this weekend that I want to feel something more in a relationship than I could ever feel for you. I didn't want to hurt you, but I planned to tell you after this weekend that we're through. I hoped you'd see it for yourself, too. With all of this, you sure made this easier for me."

"Don't believe her, Jack. She's a bitch."

"Pack your bags *now*," he snapped.

After a glance around the ballroom, Monica raised her chin. "All right, Jack. I'll go, but if you think it's over for me, you are mistaken."

"*It is over.* Why I ever believed anything you said is what I need to be held accountable for. And I owe Abby an apology."

Fury erupted in Monica's eyes. She clenched her hands, turned on her heel, and strode from the ballroom. It was a show of a lot of emotion for Monica who wasn't the type to cause a scene, or be passionate about anything other than what she would buy on her next shopping spree.

Now knowing the extent of Monica's deviousness, Jack also told his assistant to have his locks changed in Fort Lauderdale. Although he'd never given Monica a key to his condo, with these stunts she'd pulled, he couldn't trust that she hadn't stolen one.

Twenty minutes later, Jack stood on the porch with Monica as the cab pulled up next to the house. He didn't say a word as he lifted her heavy suitcases into the trunk of the car. After she slid inside, he paid the driver.

Relief and freedom burst in Jack's chest as he watched the cab travel down the long driveway toward the gates. He could move on and take the path his life should have taken before Monica had interfered.

Jack strode toward the lake to find Abby. He knew her favorite spot by then and hoped she had gone there.

She had. Relieved, he released a breath of air he'd been holding.

When he walked up behind her on the decking, she jerked around. "Jack! You scared me."

"I didn't mean to frighten you, Abby," he said softly.

Seeing her again and knowing the truth of all the lies Monica had spewed about Abby, Jack sucked in another deep breath. He realized what Monica's manipulating had done—it had torn him and Abby apart. Now, he was glad it was Abby's sweet and beautiful face he gazed upon.

Would she give him a second chance? He didn't deserve it, but he hoped she would.

Abby crossed her arms over her chest. "Jack," she grumbled, "you didn't have to chase after me to tell me I embarrassed you in front of your family. If it hadn't been for my part in the wedding, I would have gone home by now. After this weekend, you won't have to see me again. I'm quitting your company too, so you won't have to fire me."

"Why didn't you tell me that you had nothing to do with Vince Michaels?" he asked.

"Because I had no idea what Monica had done. Or what you thought. I just found out tonight that you thought I had been seeing him."

Jack swore underneath his breath. "I should have known I was being manipulated. I feel like a fool. "

A frown etched Abby's brow. "I'm sorry if I embarrassed you in front of your family and friends."

"I don't care. Monica needed to be blasted for her tricks."

"But she might sue me for taping her without her permission."

"She probably doesn't have legal grounds, but if she does..." He flicked Abby a brief smile and ran his hand down her arm. "You and I will counter sue, but don't worry at all about it. Monica was bluffing just so she'd have the last say."

Abby gaped at him for a moment, then narrowed her eyes. "I shouldn't have embarrassed you. I should have just given you the recording and not blasted it for all to hear."

"It was a bit of a shock, I admit."

"For what it's worth, I'm sorry about that," Abby said as she whirled around and strode toward the mansion.

He went after her. "Abby! Wait!"

When she turned, her eyes were wide with surprise.

He grabbed her hand. "Don't go. Better yet, come into the cottage. We need to talk."

Once inside, she pulled her hand from his and sat down on the loveseat, right in the middle so he couldn't sit beside her.

Frowning, he gazed down at her, unsure how to begin. "I have my own truths to tell. Monica has been pushing for marriage. The moment I came here… When I saw you…"

"Yeah, you looked pretty angry with me."

"No, Abby, that's not what I'm talking about. I was angry with myself, and I knew deep down that I would be making the biggest mistake of my life if I married Monica. Even before we came here, I told her I wasn't sure about us. I'd been traveling for some time. When I returned to Fort Lauderdale, I knew there had never been much of a relationship between Monica and me. I didn't want to bring her, but she insisted a wedding would put me in the mood for our own. Emotionally, I was dead inside. I never wanted to feel anything again... Until I saw you again."

"So you're not marrying her?" Abby whispered.

Jack shook his head. "I just told her we're through. I should have told her months ago that it was over. I knew my feelings for her weren't right. I just hoped she'd break it off with me after seeing how happy Miles and Carly were. Otherwise, I was going to end it after this weekend. Considering what she did to us, I shouldn't have waited or worried about her feelings."

He ran his hand through his hair. "Abby, when I thought you cheated on me, I went a little crazy. Seemed I was repeating my father's life and dooming myself to heartache if I stayed in a relationship with you. I was never going to let anyone hurt me again. Monica kept showing up at my apartment. It just seemed to me that having a girlfriend that couldn't touch my heart was better. I was going through the motions, and I didn't care who I was with."

"I never cheated on you Jack," Abby assured him. "And I'm not like your mother! I know she hurt you when she had affairs with other men."

"I feel like the biggest jerk for ever doubting you. And the baby..."

Abby said nothing. She bit her lip and stared at her hands in her lap.

"*Was mine*," he added flatly, feeling a heavy weight tugging on his heart. "You might have kept the baby, if you didn't think I was ditching you for your roommate."

She pinned him with her gaze. "What do you mean, Jack—*kept* the baby? I would have kept the baby whether you were in my life or not. I *lost* the baby in the first trimester."

He waved Abby to the side and dropped down on the loveseat beside her. "But you said it was your fault. That you were responsible..." His eyes were burning with emotion as he grabbed her shoulders. "When you came back from Europe, you were obviously not pregnant. Monica said that she'd heard that you'd *done something*, that she didn't like repeating it, but she thought I ought to know. Of course, that was all a lie, too."

"Yes, Jack. It was."

"You told me not having the baby was your fault. What did you mean?"

"I said it was my fault because it was. I was upset because you didn't want the baby, and I thought I was standing in your way with Monica. I took off for a hike in the mountains by myself, knowing I shouldn't. It began to rain." Tears trickled down her face. "I've always been such a klutz, but mostly when it came to you. I slipped on some rocks and broke my leg. I lay on the trail for hours until someone came along. I came down with pneumonia and had a miscarriage. I called you from the hospital... I thought you'd blame me for yet another one of my klutzy episodes…" Her lips turned downward. "I'm never going to have children."

Jack pulled her into his arms. "Are you sure? Is that what your doctor said?"

"No. That's not what I mean. I can physically have a baby, but how can I trust myself? What if I caused something like this to happen again?"

"Baby, it's not your fault. It was my fault for making you upset, or you wouldn't have taken off. You'll have children and be a great mother—loving, good, and kind." He took her cool face between his hands and kissed the tears on her cheeks. "We've lost two years. Damn, Monica for her lying and playing us for fools—and damn me the most. How could I not see through her lies? Seen her true character, especially?"

"She was good at setting us up. From the moment, Monica moved in with me, she told me you often looked at her in a certain way and flirted with her behind my back—and I believed her, too."

"That was a lie. I never did. I was true to you."

"And on the phone..." Abby's voice broke and she swiped away a tear. "When I was in Europe, you were so cold. You said it was over between us."

"Damn it—that was because I'd seen your bedroom and your social media page with Vince Michaels. I thought I'd seen evidence you were cheating on me."

"And I thought you wanted to break up with me to be with Monica. Now I can see how you must have been hurt when you saw those faked photos online. I knew I'd been hacked and took the pictures down and changed my password, but I had no idea that you'd seen them."

Jack shoved his hand through his hair. "And I should have asked you to explain why his things were in your room. We would have found out it was a lie, if only I had asked you."

"I left you a couple of messages on your phone when I was in the hospital to tell you what happened with the baby, but you never returned my call. I didn't think you cared. I thought you were probably relieved."

"No, Abby, I would have been there for you. Somehow, Monica must have retrieved my messages when my cell phone went missing. She must have taken it when she stopped at my condo to ask me if I'd heard from you."

Abby swiped at the tears on her face. "It was as if you'd forgotten me."

"Damn, Abby. I've never forgotten you. *Never.* Or gotten over you. That's why I was so angry at first when I saw you here for the wedding. It still hurt and I was still angry at what I thought was your betrayal."

"Jack..."

He ran his hand up her arm. She shivered beneath his

touch.

"Abby, you've always been in my dreams. My heart felt like it was ripped out." Swallowing the emotions welling inside him, Jack stood. "How can you ever forgive me? You need to find someone who deserves you. I should never have taken her word for anything to do with us."

With a heavy heart, he turned to walk away, the pain overwhelmingly unbearable that he'd lost Abby because of his own stupidity. His eyes burned.

"Jack," she called out to his back, "you didn't believe Monica over me. You believed all the evidence she set up to convince you that I was cheating."

He paused and nodded. "True. I did."

"Jack, I love you. I fell for her tricks, too. I've always loved you and I'm not getting over that fact, so you come back here right now."

Jack turned and hurried back to her. "I'd walk over hot coals if you'll just forgive me."

"I don't want you hurt anymore, even from hot coals. . . and yes let's forgive each other!" With tears running down her face, she stepped up to him. "I'll forgive you, just promise me that if anything ever looks suspicious, or bothers you, or if anyone tries to interfere in our relationship, you'll talk to me and get my side of it."

Jack pulled her into his arms. Although her eyes shone with tears, she beamed a happy smile.

He squeezed her. "Abby, I was an utter idiot to think you were cheating on me. I'm sorry for the terrible things I said to you."

"Jack, I know your mother's behavior affected you. I promise to trust you, if you'll trust me."

"I will."

She ran her hand along his jaw. "And promise me the next time we fight, we start by discussing everything. I don't want anyone else ever to come between us again. My heart can't take any more breaking."

He grinned. "Does that mean we're officially back together?"

Abby flicked him a smile and nodded. "If you want to be…"

"Does that include the rest of you?" He laid his palm on her breast. "Because I've been fighting the urge to drag you into my arms and to the nearest hotel since I first saw you this weekend."

"You've been staying with Monica."

"Only in the same room. I just got back from the Middle East, after taking as many contracts as I could to make money to buy back the company. It's been over five months since we've been together in that way. My disinterest is what drove her to push even harder for marriage or to make more of our relationship. But enough about all that. She doesn't deserve our sympathy or consideration. I hope we can put her behind us now."

Abby sucked in her breath as his hands slid over down her back and cupped her bottom. He pulled her closer to his rock-hard body that did not hide his attraction and interest. "Jack!"

He smiled and lifted her off the floor.

Abby wrapped her arms around his neck, her legs around his waist, and then she raised her lips to his. "Kiss me."

After a thorough kiss that rocked him, Jack jerked back. "I think someone is outside the front window, baby. Did you hear footsteps outside?"

Abby sighed and shook her head. "No. I wasn't listening."

On the other side of the cottage, through the windows, he heard a woman's laughter, and a man's deep voice.

"Now, I hear them, Jack."

"Yeah, it's getting to be like downtown New York here," Jack said, squeezing Abby in his arms. "Hold on. We'll go out the back door. I know a secluded place in the woods."

With her arms around his neck and her legs around his waist, Jack carried Abby along a tree-lined path that ran into a wooded area. "Hang on tight," he said.

She chuckled against his neck. "I am."

Guided by solar lights, he carried her down the path while she buried her face in his neck, sending waves of desire through him. Finally, they arrived at the gazebo, far from the main house and the cottage. Moonlight sparkled on the lake.

"We can be alone here." He sat her on top of the railing and she ran her hands up his chest muscles and wrapped her arms around his neck.

He kissed her ear then trailed kisses along her collarbone as he pushed the thin straps of her sundress off her shoulders.

"Do you know what you do to me?" he asked.

"Show me," she said in a low, sexy voice.

His pulse pounded. "Oh, I will, but first I want to see you in the moonlight." He laid his hands on her breasts and kissed the satiny skin, exposed to his view. He pulled her dress down a little further. Seeing her beauty like this, after two years without her, sent waves of excitement coursing through him. Jack lowered his lips and let his tongue delve into her cleavage and lower. He cupped her full breasts in his hands. Her skin smooth and pale glowed in the moonlight as he teased her soft rosebud nipples with his mouth and tongue. She moaned softly.

Jack groaned and returned his lips to hers. He kissed her with all the pent-up passion he'd suppressed for two years.

He molded his hands on her breasts again. "Perhaps we shouldn't do this here." He trailed kisses down her throat. "Because I want to get you out of your clothes, all of them."

She sighed. "Probably not the place, but I don't want you to stop."

Jack kissed her again in a deep, thorough kiss. Then he lifted his mouth from hers, his breathing heavy. "All I want to do is get inside you, but I have a feeling we should go back to the house."

"Kiss me first." She cupped his head and pulled him back to her. When their lips touched again, any thoughts he had about leaving blew away with the fragrant summer breeze.

He moved his hands to cradle the base of her skull and lowered his lips to her throat. He kissed his way to her breasts and taut nipples. She sighed.

Then he slid his fingers between her satiny-smooth thighs. Touching her intimately through her panties, he found her most sensitive spot.

She moaned. "Now I'm sure I can't wait until we get back to the house."

"You always did drive me senseless. We're probably okay though," he said with a low chuckle. "Who besides us would want to come out here this late at night?"

"No one, Jack." She flattened her hands on his chest. "You're the only one who has ever made me feel this way."

"Like out of control?"

She laughed. "Yeah, way out of control. And I've never done this with anyone but you."

"Abby, I'm sorry about everything. I'm sorry we lost so much time. I don't want to lose any more."

She flung her long hair back, allowing him access to her neck. It spilled down her back and he kissed her neck, her ears, and her mouth. She shivered in his arms and he could feel her excitement.

He bent and slid her panties down her legs and over her strappy high-heeled sandals, letting his fingers touch her sleek warm skin.

He rose up and stood between her parted thighs and pulled her against his hard erection.

"What if we're discovered?" he choked out, his last line of defense.

"What's the chance of that?"

"*Mmmmmm.*" He exhaled a long sigh as he caressed her intimately with his fingers. "A million to one, you think?"

"*Ahhh.*" She moaned against his lips. "Perhaps zero chance that anyone would come out here, so I think we're safe."

He unzipped his pants and pressed his erection between her thighs.

Jack kissed her bared neck. "We *are* deep in the woods..."

He reached into his pocket and for his wallet and retrieved a condom. With shaky hands, he ripped oven the package and sheathed himself. He pushed inside her welcoming warmth, and cupping her bottom, he sank into her even deeper as he thrust to be closer.

Her body tightened around him caused waves of

excitement to course through him and pleasure like fire in his loins.

"This is...what...we both need," he said as he drove into her over and over again.

When her body clenched around him with her release, he went over the edge with her. His world reeled and his climax was explosive.

"Oh, damn," he said, into the curve of her neck. After several minutes, he blew out a deep breath, and chuckled under his breath. "What you do to me is insane. Even after that, all I want to do is get you alone again and to kiss you senseless. I'm not complaining though. I'd rather have a little insanity in my life than live without you." He wrapped his arms around her. "That was incredible. You're incredible."

Abby pressed her face to his cheek and chuckled. "Just like old times."

Jack raised his head and sighed. "I hope I didn't hurt you."

"No. I enjoyed every moment."

"I've missed you." He gave her a thorough kiss. Then Jack lifted her off the railing and set her feet on the ground. He pulled up his pants, while she slipped on her panties.

"Let's go somewhere that's more private," he said.

"You can stay with me in my room tonight."

As they walked along the path back toward the house, hand in hand, they didn't notice the rustling in the bushes or the paper cup that had been crushed and pitched to the ground only moments earlier.

* * *

They entered the mansion by the side entrance to the kitchen, Abby was a little nervous as they made their way to her room. They slipped past everyone that they knew well, but then ran into Mr. James Farrington at the bottom of the backstairs. Abby bit her lip.

"Jack, were you outside near the boathouse? Did you see anything strange?" Jack's Uncle James asked. "Trent told me one of the boats is missing."

Jack shook his head. "No. I didn't notice anything."

"Oh, well, maybe someone just has the boat out late tonight," Mr. Farrington said, but he looked worried. "We'll have to check in the morning."

Abby and Jack reassured him, then continued to the second floor.

They ran into Jack's Aunt Gertrude in the hallway. She smirked at them as if she caught them with their hands in the candy dish. "Just look at you two."

Abby's eyes widened when she thought of what his elderly aunt must think. And rightly so. One glance at Jack and she wondered if she looked as disheveled from their romp in the woods as he did. His hair stuck up in the front and his shirttail was partially out of his pants. Abby gave Jack's aunt a faint smile in passing and resisted straightening her clothing, or patting her hair into place as they walked by.

Then Jack's Uncle Peter stuck his head out of one of the guest rooms. "Oh, Jack... I see you're going to bed...you and Abby together. Well, goodnight."

"Goodnight, Uncle Peter." Jack took a blushing Abby's hand and ushered her down the hallway. He muttered near Abby's ear. "See why I thought the woods was better? Not that I care—only for your sake—but by tomorrow morning the news will be all over this house that we're staying together."

She squeezed Jack's hand. "I don't care if you don't."

When she was with him, the world faded away. Even

though she wanted them to have a deep love, if he didn't feel the same depths of emotion that she felt for him, this would be enough. He did care for her and he wasn't getting away this time. She would work harder and make him love her.

Once they were inside Abby's bedroom in the mansion, and the door locked, Jack turned to face her. The smile on his face sent happiness overflowing inside her. Never, ever, had she believed his eyes might hold such tenderness for her again, or that they could ever get back together. She stepped into his warm embrace. He leaned back against the door and crushed her against him.

She had missed him so much... Abby pressed her hands and face to his chest, her emotions overwhelming. "I never want to let you go, Jack."

"I'll never let you." Jack cupped her chin and raised her face to his. "God, I love your mouth, Abby."

He lowered his mouth to hers and filled her senses. Their tongues entwined. Her toes curled as he plundered her lips once again. Although they had made love less than thirty minutes ago, their kisses quickly turned fiery again.

Heat rushed to her core and her nipples tightened. She moaned her desire.

When they came up for air, Abby pressed her cheek to his chest. Drawing in a deep breath, she raised her face to his.

"I've never stopped loving you from that first time I saw you in high school. It was love at first sight for me. It may sound ridiculous, but it's the truth. I love you, Jack."

He cupped her jaw. "You were always special to me." He smiled with such warmth in his eyes, a thrill shot through her. While he had not exactly returned her words of love—in that moment, she was certain he cared for her.

"I don't think I'll ever get enough of you, Abby."

He crushed his lips to hers once more. He kissed her thoroughly, delighting her senses. He moved his mouth to kiss her ears.

With shaky hands, she pulled his shirttail out of his pants and ran her hands up his muscular chest to touch his smooth, warm skin.

He sighed and leaned his chin against the top of her head. "You smell so good."

"So do you."

Jack groaned, then he tipped up her chin. "Abby, I feel like ripping your clothes off, but I'll restrain myself—although making love in the moonlight didn't satisfy enough of my need to see you."

He ran his hands along her shoulders, pushing down the straps of her sundress, and turning her to unzip her dress. Her legs were shaking and her entire body trembled with anticipation.

"I haven't seen you in so long. I want every bit of you," he said hoarsely.

He pulled the dress over her head, unsnapped her bra, and slid her panties down her legs.

When she stood for him completely naked, she felt exposed. He unbuttoned the top buttons of his shirt, but ripped off the last in his haste to get out of it. She tugged at his belt and he helped her undo his pants.

When he was naked, she stepped into his arms and cupped him, touching and stroking.

Jack groaned and grabbed her wrists and took a long gaze at her body. Then he swept her up into his arms. He yanked back the comforter and deposited her on the cool sheets.

He stood back for a moment. "I've missed you, Abby. What a fool I have been. You're beautiful inside and out. I should have seen through Monica's lies and the manipulations."

Then Jack joined her on the bed. His rough palm scraped over her breasts, his thumbs finding her nipples and making them hard, sending hot desire through her. "I think we're going to burn up the sheets before this night is over, but I'm trying to control the fire."

His mouth captured hers in a hungry kiss. Then he was touching her everywhere, loving her, and stoking the flames even hotter.

"I want you, Jack. I can't wait any longer."

"All right." She heard the rip of a condom package, then he lay beside her and rolled on top of her and between her thighs. He entered her slowly, then thrust deeper, surging to take his own pleasure yet taking enough time to make sure she peaked, too.

Abby held on to him as each powerful thrust made her reach higher. She climaxed and cried out her fierce pleasure as her body tightened around him.

"*Damn. Damn. Damn.*" Shuddering, he exploded inside her.

Jack fell back on his back, then gathered her in his arms. "Incredible," he whispered. Then he grinned and sighed.

After a while, their breathing returned to normal.

She raised her fingers to brush strands of hair from his perspiring forehead.

So much for going slower," he muttered into her ear. His roughened jaw scraped her cheek. "You drive me wild, Abby. You always have."

"It was perfect and I'm glad we took precautions, Jack."

"I wouldn't care anyway. Whatever happens, happens. You're mine and you're never getting away, so get used to the idea."

She chuckled. "Something like a business takeover?"

"Exactly. And you're one hot commodity."

"I don't think we should risk another pregnancy because you wouldn't want to get one of your employees pregnant… It wouldn't look good at the company."

"You? *As just one of my employees?*" He laughed. "I never thought I wanted kids, because I had to help raise my brothers while my mother was out running around. Hell, I didn't find out for certain my father was my father until I was twenty-one and had a DNA test. But, Abby, I want you to have my baby, but only when you're ready."

"You do?"

He grasped Abby's shoulders and looked deeply in her eyes. "Don't you know that I love you? I had been getting used to the idea of us being a family when all that happened."

"Jack! Say that again."

"I said I had been getting used to the idea. On that awful day that tore us apart, I was bringing over a surprise present for you to make amends, baby things and a teddy bear in a big basket—"

"Oh, that's so sweet of you, but no! I meant the other part, Jack. The part where you said you *loved* me. You've never said it before."

Jack frowned and looked surprised. "Of course, I've said it. Hundreds of times."

She shook her head. "No, Jack. You've said you *desired me*. That I *meant so much to you*, but you never said the words *I love you*. Believe me, those words I would have remembered."

He reached out and stroked her cheek. "Oh, Abby, I've been an even bigger fool than I thought if I made you insecure about my love for you. I've always loved you, beyond my wildest expectations of what love is. Sorry I've never said it to you before like that. I was so wrapped up...working hard, and I was insensitive."

"And though you were preoccupied, I'm happy you got the company back. And *I* love you, too. Ah, it feels like the best of the old times to be with you again."

Jack held Abby in his arms as they rested against the pillows. "I'll love you forever! I think I was in love with you from that first moment we met, too. I think you were right all along about this destiny thing."

"Of course, I was right," she said, flipping him a smile, before sobering. "And may I ask? How did you end up with Monica if you weren't with her when I was in Europe?"

"Like I started to explain before, as for Monica, getting into my life—she was always showing up after you and I broke up. Months went by and I was just going through the motions of living, digging myself into my work. She followed me to Florida and got an apartment near mine. Then she started showing up at my condo, saying she wanted us to be *friends* because she was new in town. Then one night she came over and said she had to tell me that Vince Michaels and you were taking a trip. That it sounded serious between you two. I drank heavily that night..."

Abby gasped. "Another one of her lies!"

"And she didn't just say it. She had Vince back her up. She called him on his cell and he said he couldn't wait for his trip with you. She must have paid him…"

Abby frowned. "No wonder you believed her. She was the one sleeping with Vince, not me. I don't know why he did it though, except that when he visited her he was always flirting and trying to come on to me, and I rejected him. Maybe he wanted a bit of revenge on me, and that's why he helped her with her dirty tricks. I'm sure he thought it was funny to get back at me." Abby blew out a disgusted breath. "And it worked, Jack. You and I, as a couple, were nearly destroyed forever."

CHAPTER NINE

That Saturday afternoon, classical music floated through the air and reverberated through the garden. Chairs were arranged on either side of a center aisle and led to where the minister would hold the wedding ceremony beneath a canopy of red and white roses.

Jack met Abby at the rear of the mansion to wait with the other attendants for the guests to be seated and the *Wedding March* to begin.

He took in Abby's appearance. In a scarlet bridesmaid's gown with her breasts swelling above the lace-trimmed, low neckline, she took his breath away. Her long blond hair was down, though partially swept up in the back with a ribbon.

She carried a bouquet of red and white roses and smiled up at him. "Hi, Jack."

"Hello," he whispered as a rush of desire swept through him. "You are beautiful beyond words."

"You're handsome in your black tux."

He grinned and leaned in and grazed her cheek with his lips. Her perfume and the smell of roses wafted in the gentle breeze. He wanted to bury his face in the low neckline of her gown. He smiled to himself at the thought of getting her out of that red dress later tonight.

And he had a burning question to ask her…

Jack pulled her aside and smiled down at her. "I want us to be next, Abby," he whispered.

Her eyes widened. "Next for what?"

He chuckled. "What do you think? I want you to marry me. Will you? After Miles and Carly's wedding, I'll get down on my knee and make it official, and then I'll do even more to make it perfect...tonight..."

She raised a beaming face to his—the face of a beautiful woman in love. "Is that a promise?" she teased.

"This very evening…near the end of the party so we don't take anything away from Carly and Miles' gathering." He raised her hand to his lips. "I don't want to live without you any longer. I love you beyond what I ever thought love could be."

Tears shone in her eyes. "And I'll be saying yes. I want to marry you."

"I'm glad. We could go to the courthouse on Monday, but after seeing what Carly and Miles have here...with family and friends looking on, I thought you might want Uncle James to host our wedding as well."

"I'd love that. I've always wanted a big, romantic wedding."

"I thought so. And I want you to have the wedding of your dreams. You deserve it. You'll be the most beautiful bride ever. I can't wait to make you mine—to commit to you forever."

"I am yours now, Jack."

"I'm glad to hear it." Jack pulled Abby into his arms and sighed with contentment. "We will have the big house, the land, the horses, whatever you want. I can afford it now. However, I want the wedding soon because I don't want to chance losing you again. You might have married someone else with what Monica did to us. I could have lost you forever—to Sam or to someone else."

When Jack's jacket rubbed the lace on her dress, he remembered how they'd gotten caught together two nights ago. He released her. "I guess we should watch the clothes, huh?"

She smiled. "Yes, and the makeup."

Jack was content to hold her hand—for now. Being with her again seemed like a dream. Happiness overwhelmed him.

"Jack!"

He turned to see his Uncle James waving him over. Standing with the elderly man was Uncle Peter. They seemed to be in a heated discussion.

Jack kissed Abby's cheek. "I'll return in a minute, Abby."

He crossed to his uncles, not in the mood to hear his younger uncle's grumblings about his taking over McAlister. They went off to the side of the gathered crowd where they could talk privately.

Uncle James flicked his gaze to his other uncle. "Jack, it seems your Uncle Peter has a beef with us."

"I do. First, you have it all, James. You gobble up companies...people. Take away their livelihoods...their homes."

"That's unfair," James said in a steely voice. "I had nothing to do with your gambling debts, which caused you to lose this house. Or your mismanagement that caused you to lose McAlister Construction. I bought the estate because it was Eliza's home, and I didn't want it destroyed so a developer could build five hundred houses on the land."

Uncle Peter ran a hand through his dark curly hair in

frustration. "And what about Jack?"

"You should be glad he brought the company back into the family," James added. "And it was already lost to you several years ago."

Uncle Peter's shoulders drooped. "But this makes me look bad..."

Jack blew out a deep breath. "I didn't buy back the company to make you look bad, Uncle Peter. The business had been in our family for generations, and when the opportunity came up, I wanted it back."

Uncle Peter's eyes darted away behind his black-framed glasses. "I suppose I can't blame anyone but myself for my failures."

Jack could tell he was still upset. "Don't be angry with me, or too hard on yourself," Jack said, trying to sooth the man.

Uncle Peter shrugged. "I suppose not. You know I'm not the only one who is hurt by this action... And I'll give you a business tip, Jack—watch your back around your competitors—especially Ansen Burns, if you have any dealings with him."

"Thank you." That was the second time he'd been warned about Ansen Burns. The first time was by Sam Preston.

Uncle Peter walked away.

Jack turned to his Uncle James. "I only hope he will come to accept the situation."

"He will, Jack, but one thing he said that is true, when one becomes successful, one always has to watch his back around his competition. From what I hear, Ansen Burns might be someone you should be careful around. Even more so, since if he does anything, he'll just hire someone to do his dirty work."

Jack nodded in agreement. "I've heard this too many times *not* to pay attention about Burns, so I'll take the warning."

* * *

Abby thought Jack looked handsome in his black tux with the crisp white shirt and bow tie as he strode across the lawn to meet his uncles. Contented that they would be married, Abby smiled to herself.

"Abby!" Sam strode up to her, his sharp tone startling her. He dropped his gaze to her breasts. Then Sam fisted one hand.

Abby shrank back as he stood over her, his anger sizzling beneath his less-than-friendly expression. She raised her chin, but a chill ran along her spine. "Oh, hi, Sam. I thought you might be with your stepfather."

"No, Ralph couldn't make the wedding. But I leave for two days... I come back here to find out that you've ditched me, and that Jack and you are back together," Sam snarled. "How did I not see this coming?"

Even if Sam was angry, she had nothing to fear. He wouldn't dare strike out at her with so many people around.

"Sam, stop it. I told you I think of you as a friend, and nothing more. I never meant to hurt you. I am sorry if I did."

"But I thought… That you and me..."

"No, Sam. I tried to tell you before. I've known you for a long time, and I think of you as a friend. A good friend. I never said I would date you. I only told you I would consider it."

"So you used me to make Jack jealous—to take him back from Monica. And on the boating trip, was that a phony fall?"

"No. And I did not use you, Sam! Listen to me, I've always loved Jack."

His face reddened and Sam took a step back. "All right, Abby, if that's how it's going to be…" Sam darted his eyes away. "Don't expect me to ask you out again." Then he strode away.

Sam's anger frightened her and Abby blew out a deep breath of relief when Jack headed in her direction.

Jack's brows drew into a worried frown. "Sam looked like he was bothering you. What did he say to upset you?"

The *Wedding March* began.

"Everything is okay. I'll tell you later."

Jack gave her a hesitant glance and a nod before he strode to the front to stand by the waiting groom.

Abby hoped Sam would eventually understand, but she put thoughts of him away because it was time to begin.

Abby walked down the aisle with the other bridal attendants and took her place up front.

When Jack caught her gaze, she felt love flow between them. Now, they would be the next to marry, even though misunderstandings and tricks had nearly ruined their lives.

Carly's father had passed away years ago, so Mr. James Farrington escorted her down the aisle. Carly made a gorgeous bride as she walked with him toward her groom.

Happiness welled inside Abby for her friend and for herself. She would be doing this soon.

After the ceremony, photographers snapped endless photos of the newlyweds and their attendants. When the posing was finished, everyone proceeded toward the reception to meet up with guests in the glittering ballroom.

For dinner, Abby and the other bridesmaids were

assigned seats on Carly's side of the long wedding party table, while all the male attendants were seated on Miles's side.

Jack linked his arm with Abby's and pulled her aside. He stared down at her for a moment, and then released her with a sigh. "It looks like we're going to be separated for this part of the reception, Abby. I'm having trouble letting you go. Seems this having to leave you has become a recurring event."

Then he escorted her to the wedding party table that took center stage in the ballroom and pulled out the chair beside Carly for her.

After Abby sat, Jack put his hand on her shoulder and squeezed. "Until later, sweetheart," he whispered in her ear. Then he turned to go and took his seat on the other side of Miles.

Dinner was delicious with several choices: Filet Mignon, Beef Wellington, Pan-seared Red Snapper, and Lobster Thermidor was served. Expensive champagne flowed like water.

After dinner, several servers wheeled out the huge wedding cake.

In the midst of all the 'ohs' and 'ahs,' one of the doors swung open. Monica walked in, carrying a baseball bat.

Abby's heart pounded as Monica walked toward the wedding party's table. Crooked under her arm, she carried a laptop.

Jack rose from the table. "Monica, didn't I send you off in a cab yesterday?"

CHAPTER TEN

A snarl on her face—as much as one could have with all her cosmetic work—Monica approached the wedding party table. "I decided that I wasn't through... That we weren't through, Jack."

Jack didn't like the look in her eyes one bit. He stood up, looked at his cousins who were poised to jump to action, and held out his hands to stop them. "I'll handle this, guys."

He turned back to Monica. "You shouldn't have come back here. Now put the bat down. And by the looks of the case, I'm assuming that's my laptop. Set it down gently," he demanded.

"All right." She held out the laptop and let it drop straight to the floor. "Is that gentle enough for you?" Then she stomped her high-heeled shoe on top and tried to grind the computer into the ground.

Jack considered jumping over the table to get to her. "Stop it, Monica," he suggested with deadly calm.

"Not until I'm finished." Monica took the bat and whacked the computer, cracking the case. "Now the next hit is for Carly, for interfering with my relationship with you, Jack. And I know she did."

Monica swung at the cake that time and icing splashed on everyone within twenty feet of it.

Jack moved around the long table and toward her. "Monica, that's enough. Put the bat down," he said in a threatening tone.

"No, not until I'm *finished*," she repeated. Monica stepped toward Abby. "You should see your rental car, Jack. Now, take your last look at Abby's face."

Jack lunged toward Monica. He grabbed her and held her arms to her sides until Monica dropped the bat.

"I hate her," Monica cried.

"Should we call the police?" someone suggested from behind them.

Jack shook his head. "No, I can handle this." He shook her. "Monica, do you want to get into trouble? You could go to jail."

She struggled in his arms. "Let me go."

"Monica, Abby didn't come between us," Jack said. "I know I couldn't have gone through with the engagement you wanted. Deep down inside, I hoped you'd realize, if you came here with me, that we weren't right together—just by seeing how happy Carly and Miles are. We never had that—well, truthfully, we never had much of anything. I hoped that, combined with how much you hate cold weather, you would want to break it off with me."

Monica sputtered. "If she had never been in the picture, you would have loved me. *I want her to pay for this*," she spat out.

Jack held on to her tightly. "I never stopped loving Abby, and I'm not going to. You are the reason we broke up in the first place, Monica. You interfered in our relationship with your fabricated lies. You made me think she was cheating on me with your little schemes. And if you try to hurt Abby, I will make you regret it."

All the tension went out of Monica's body. "But—"

"There are no buts and no more lies and betrayals. I love Abby. I always have and always will. You need to understand and accept that."

Monica's mouth turned downward. "What will I do without you?"

Abby stepped forward. "You'll find someone else in Florida. Or perhaps Vince Michaels is still available? He deserves someone like you."

Jack released Monica's arms. "Monica, you had a relationship with him and tried to lay the blame on Abby." He raised an eyebrow. "Besides, my life is with Abby, where it would already have been if you hadn't interfered."

Jack turned to Abby, Carly and his uncle. "Is it okay if she leaves here? Abby? Carly—she ruined your cake? And, Uncle James, she's on your property? I'll call a cab to take her to the airport, but that's all up to you. The alternative is to call the police and have her arrested."

Uncle James said he was all right with Monica leaving.

Carly nodded. "She's trying to ruin my reception, but I'm okay as long as she goes—now.

Visibly shaken, Abby crossed her arms over her chest and raised her chin. "Okay, let Monica go, but only if this time she doesn't come back."

Jack gazed down at Monica. "If you leave now, I won't prosecute you for damaging the rental car… But don't make me regret it."

A young man strode in with a large box with a lid and a big silver bow. "Special delivery for the wedding party from a *Mr. James Farrington*—a gift for the bride, to be opened by the best man."

He placed the box on the table to the right of Miles the

groom, and in front of where Jack would have been sitting if he hadn't moved away from his spot at the table. *Strange*.

The deliveryman pulled out a piece of paper. "I'm supposed to make this announcement: Roses are red, violets are blue, you have this coming, I hope you enjoy it, too."

"Hold on," Uncle James bellowed from across the room. "I didn't send that package."

Abby's face paled. "Jack, the box is ticking. And it was meant for you." She picked up the box. Gasps sounded around the room.

Jack's heart raced. "Be careful not to drop it, Abby. It might be a bomb."

"I know," she squeaked. "I'll just take it out of the room."

Abby slowly moved across the room on unsteady legs, in high heels and with the box clutched in her arms.

When Jack reached her, he took the package from her. "No, Abby, I'd better be the one to do that." He ran out of the room with the box.

He heard Abby shout from behind him, "Be careful, Jack!"

As he proceeded out of the house and across the lawn, Jack noticed his male cousins ran after the guy who had delivered the present. He saw Chris tackle the kid to the ground.

Jack kept on walking, across the patio, past the swimming pool, and onto the lawn. He paused, hoping he was far enough away from everyone. Then he lobbed the package as if it were a football, hoping it would land as far away as it could from several old oak trees and the pool house. Then he headed in the opposite direction.

Over his shoulder, Jack watched and held his breath as

the package soared through the air. The box plummeted to the ground. *Thump.* He waited. Nothing happened, certainly not the explosion he'd expected.

One of his elderly aunts said from behind him, "I just hope that wasn't an expensive Waterford clock, Gertrude."

"*Tsk, tsk,* Beatrice. I hope not too," replied Aunt Gertrude. "You didn't tell me that one of our handsome nephews was paranoid—or that he could be so dramatic either."

The box began to tick louder. Jack held his breath again. The lid popped open and out of the package burst party streamers, which littered the lawn for several yards. A Jack-in-the-box sprang out.

Jack stared at the gift and ran his hand through his hair. He felt like the biggest fool. It had just been a gag.

* * *

Puzzled, but relieved there hadn't been an explosion, Jack strode across the lawn to more closely check out the package. He bent down and tried to see what they were dealing with.

Inside was a wind up clock, which had been ticking and had probably set off the springs to eject the top lid of the box.

Abby rushed up to him. "Why would someone do this, Jack?"

He shook his head. "I don't know."

A few people laughed behind him.

Another male guest chuckled. "A prank on you, McAlister. He put it right in front of your chair at the table."

"Very funny, isn't it?" Jack said dryly.

"Let's go back to the party," someone else said behind them. "It's just a big joke."

Those who had gathered on the lawn returned to the ballroom and Jack and Abby were left alone.

Frowning, he straightened up and looked at Abby, shaking his head.

"Joke, Jack?" Abby asked. "A *Jack-in-the-box*? Too big of a coincidence that the gift represents your name, don't you think?"

"Or is it *really* just a stupid prank to disturb the wedding celebration?"

A worried look flitted across Abby's face. "Other than Monica, Jack, who would want to ruin Carly's reception?"

"Abby, I should have told you before it could possibly be someone who is angry that I'm taking over McAlister. We've had some warnings. I don't know how serious the threat is."

"Who?"

He shook his head just as Uncle James joined them on the lawn.

"So what is it, Jack?" the elderly man asked.

"I don't know. Maybe just a prank. What do you think?" Jack asked, wanting to get the older man's opinion.

"I'm not sure who would do this to disrupt the reception either," his uncle said. "But I wonder if it is something more..."

"I do, too." Jack bent down again and examined the card on the package. "No name, which was to be expected."

Just then, Chris, Alex, and Trent dragged back the delivery boy. He couldn't have been more than sixteen years old.

"But I didn't do anything wrong," the young man complained.

Abby frowned. "He's just a kid."

"I doubt Monica had time to put this together." Jack turned to the young man. "We just want to ask you some questions. Who sent this package and why the poem?"

The boy shook his head. "I don't know who he was. He came into the florist shop yesterday and asked me to deliver this box for him as a side job. I did exactly as he instructed—presented the present and set it on the table next to the groom. In front of the Best Man. Then, I read the poem as he instructed. And he paid me well—with cash."

Uncle James's brow furrowed. "This is eerily suspicious, Jack. There are a couple of people who come to mind who might dislike you and me at the moment."

"Yeah, one is Uncle Peter," Jack grumbled. "He seems upset with me."

Uncle James shook his head. "I don't think your uncle would do anything harmful."

Jack narrowed his eyes. "Then what about construction companies, my competition in this area?"

"Both Ansen Burns and Ralph Preston have the most to lose from you buying McAlister Construction. However, Preston's my friend and he's a nice man. I don't believe he'd do anything like this. He was supposed to be here tonight, but he called and cancelled. Said he wasn't feeling well..."

Jack frowned. "When we first arrived, I talked to Preston's nephew Sam on the boat. Sam seemed angry when he knew we would be competitors in business, and then he dropped it. And *Sam Preston* is here at the wedding." Jack turned to the teen. "Sam Preston has dark, reddish-brown hair and some freckles. Does this fit the description?"

The kid nodded. "Yeah, that sounds like him."

"Thanks," Jack said.

"Young man, after you give us your contact info, you can go," Uncle James said.

Abby stepped closer to Jack. "Do you think Sam is still here?"

"Alex, would you go inside the house and see if he is?" Jack asked. "It might have been him, but we can't be sure."

Now the only ones on the lawn with Jack, were Uncle James, Abby, Trent and Chris.

And then there was Monica, who strode up to join them.

Jack's patience with her was running out. "Why haven't you called a cab, Monica?" he snapped.

Monica shrugged. "I wasn't quite ready to leave."

Jack folded his arms over his chest. "Maybe I should convince you. You know that with what you did inside, and what you did to my laptop and rental car, you're skating on thin ice even to be here. I should call the police right now."

Monica jutted her chin toward him. "But you said you wouldn't!"

"I said I wouldn't call them on the condition that you leave—and you're still here," Jack said in a steely voice. "If I were you, I wouldn't bet on no police intervention, so don't push me, Monica."

Abby moved up to them. "Yeah, why are you still here, Monica? Leave while you still can. There are lots of witnesses, and I could have you arrested for threatening me with a bat."

Monica made an ugly face.

Uncle James's diminutive English Butler, Beasley, hurried out of the house, headed in their direction. "Mr. Farrington, your study has been ransacked and the safe broken into."

Uncle James turned to his grandson. "Call the police, Trent. I'll speak to security."

Mr. Farrington and his butler headed for the mansion.

Jack, Trent, Chris, and Abby took a look around the lawn and backyard, with Monica following behind them.

When they neared the patio and pool house, Abby stopped in her tracks. "I think it has to be Sam who broke into the safe. He told me he stayed in the house one night, instead of going back to his hotel room. Now looking back, I think he could have used the opportunity to check out the house."

"I saw Sam upstairs, when he pretended to be coming out of your room, Abby," Jack said, swearing under his breath. "He was probably snooping to see if he could get to the safe. Well, at least we have an idea who might be responsible. He won't be hard to catch. He's probably still on the grounds. When the police get here—"

Sam rushed from behind the pool house and grabbed Abby's arm. "You betrayed me, Abby," he snarled. "Don't call the police, or I'll shoot her. I know she means something to you, Jack, so I'll take Abby with me, to hurt you—and to keep you from coming after me."

"Let Abby go, Sam," Jack demanded, fear soaring within him. "What do you have against me?

"I expected to inherit Preston Construction and his money. Now Ralph tells me his business isn't doing well, and with McAlister being taken over by you, he's already lost a few of his best clients, who want to drop him and sign with you. If this keeps up, he'll have to file for bankruptcy. We were already in trouble..." Sam pressed the gun harder against Abby's head and her face paled. "I was his heir—his VP! So I'm taking some cold hard cash, gold coins and jewels to make up for it. What I took is a pittance to James Farrington, and you all owe me. My stepfather owes me... And Abby owes me."

"I don't owe you anything," Abby retorted.

Sam hauled her toward the parked cars.

"Sam," Jack ground out, "if anyone's running your stepfather's business into the ground, it's you." Jack's gaze dropped to Sam's overfilled pockets. They weighed him down.

If Sam tried to run, Jack would have the advantage. "You're not going to get away with this, Sam. I've done nothing but buy back my family's business. All this mismanagement was happening to your company before I even got here. And you couldn't stand the idea of more competition. Now, put the gun down."

Sam's face turned bright red. "And have the police haul me away? If I'm going to jail, I'm giving you misery, too. Abby's going with me or else."

"Don't hurt her," Jack ordered.

Abby twisted in Sam's grip. "Sam, don't do this."

"Don't try to resist, Abby, or I'll have to hurt you. You're going with me." Sam thrust the gun below her jaw. She ceased struggling.

Monica crossed her arms over her chest. "Yes, Sam, do her in while you're at it," she urged.

Icy fear curled around Jack's heart. "Shut up, Monica," he snapped. "Sam, let Abby go and go it alone."

Sam hauled Abby toward his car, which was parked nearby, obviously placed there to make his getaway easier. "Don't call the cops or come after us."

* * *

Sam gripped Abby's arm as he yanked her toward his

getaway car parked near the pool house. She tripped on her gown, and stumbled. He caught her and pulled her behind him. He yanked open his car door, shoved her inside and across to the passenger side, and took his own seat. He flung the car in reverse and then into drive. The tires squealed out of the parking area as Sam drove the car away.

"There is no way you can make me stay with you."

Sam snarled. "You'll stay with me long enough for me to find out what I was missing, and for Jack to at least feel a token of what I feel—his life in an upheaval."

He was driving too fast and Abby put on her seatbelt. "Where are you taking me?"

"Canada, now that everything has gone wrong. My stepfather found out... Never mind. I didn't plan to run, but I'm glad I was prepared if it came down to this."

"Let me out of the car now and just go on your way."

"Not a chance. I'd never get away with this without you as security. You're my hostage."

A few minutes later, he glanced in the rear-view mirror. "Damn them—they're following us. I guess Jack doesn't believe I'd kill you."

Abby glanced over her shoulder. In the distance, through the dusk of the early evening, she saw the headlights of a car exiting the mansion's parking area, right behind them.

"Of course, Jack will follow us," she retorted. "He and his cousins aren't going to let you get away with stealing from their uncle, or taking me like this."

"We'll see." With white-knuckled fingers on the steering wheel, Sam drove the car, and the trees whirled past them.

Seeing how desperate Sam was, she pleaded, "Please let me go, and just leave Mr. Farrington's money. You'll get away—"

"Shut up, Abby. They'd arrest me in a minute. All I have to do is get to Canada. Didn't figure gold and jewelry would be so heavy, but I couldn't resist taking as much as I could stuff into my pockets. This loot will make it possible for me to live in style, outside the country."

He patted his bulging pockets and adjusted his jacket. His gun slid from his thigh to the edge of the seat, very near Abby.

With her heart pounding, she sucked in her breath and grabbed the gun. She aimed at Sam's chest. "Don't make me shoot you, Sam. Now pull over."

"Put that down," he ordered.

"No. Pull over. We're still on McAlister land. If you'll let me out, I'll walk back to the house, and you can go on your way."

With his free hand, Sam reached out and tried to grab the pistol. "Give me the damn gun, Abby."

Her hands shook uncontrollably, yet Abby kept the gun aimed, as steady as she could, on him. "I'm not going to shoot you, Sam. Now pull over."

Suddenly, the gun fired off with more force and power than she thought possible. Sam screeched and the bullet slugged into the driver's door.

"You just shot me in the thigh, Abby! Damn it! You said you wouldn't shoot me and now you've grazed me with a bullet."

"I didn't mean to. It just went off. I just want out of this car. *Now stop*."

Blood oozed from a slit the bullet had made in his pants. "You could've killed me." He wrenched the gun from her hand.

"I wish I had hurt you worse. I always knew there was something about you that I didn't like."

The distraction caused Sam to lose control of the vehicle and they veered off the driveway. Metal screeched as they sideswiped a tree before slamming to an abrupt stop.

Stunned, and with her heart pounding, Abby looked around to see the damage after the airbags deflated. The car had landed butted up against a tree on the passenger side, preventing her from making an escape.

Sam swung open his door. "Damn it, Abby. What am I going to do now?" He swiped his hand though his hair. Then he grasped her by the arm and hauled her out through the driver's side. "Let's go. I'm not going to be arrested. So Jack had better back off if he wants to see you alive again. If anyone tries to take me out, you're going with me."

They took off on foot with him half dragging her. Her high heels sank into the grass as he pulled her along with him.

"Take off the shoes," he ordered.

"You'd go faster without me, Sam."

"Shut up! Take off the shoes. I need my hostage."

Reluctantly, she kicked off her high heels and went with him.

"I have one of the small boats beached over here from last night. If we can reach it, we might be able to hunker down at the cabin on the island, and then get out of here tomorrow."

Fury rose in Abby. "So you were using the cabin to sneak onto the grounds of the mansion at night? I thought I'd caught that creepy guy outside by the docks, but it was you. You're the real creep. The day I fell on the island, the reason you weren't behind me on the trail, was because you'd gone to the cabin, wasn't it? You probably went to hide something there, in case Jack went to check out the cabin that day."

"So what? And that's where we're going now."

"I'm not going with you."

"Oh, yeah. You'll come with me, if I have to tie you up." He dragged her. "So shut up. I need you as a hostage, and we're going to make it to that boat."

Sam pulled her along the path that ran beside the lake. When he paused to readjust the gold in his pockets, he had to take his hands off her for a moment. Taking the opportunity for freedom, she shoved against his side, trying to knock him into the lake.

However, to her dismay, Sam grasped her shoulder. They both tumbled into the lake with a splash that sent shock waves through Abby when they plunged under the cold water.

Frantically, she kicked to the surface. She gulped in a deep breath, but her long gown made it nearly impossible to swim. A car's headlights swept the area. It had to be Jack. He must have seen the wrecked car, but with the evening dusk turning ever darker, would anyone see them in the water?

Sam caught her shoulders in a painful grip as she tried to reach the shore. He dragged her under in an attempt to pull himself out of the water. They flailed about. Panic rushed through her veins, though Abby managed to fight him off and get to the surface for more air.

"Let go of me," she cried. "Take the gold out of your pockets. It's pulling you under. You're going to drown us both."

Sam clasped her again. "I can't."

"Jack!" she cried just before Sam pulled her underwater

again. Her lungs seemed to be crushed and she gulped water this time.

Moments later, someone pulled her away from Sam's hold. *Jack.* After sputtering for air, Abby was finally able to breathe again as Jack swam and dragged her back to shore.

"Are you all right?" he asked.

She nodded, gasping for air.

"Chris, make sure she's okay." Jack handed her to his cousin who had stepped down the bank to give her a hand.

Abby collapsed on the shore. Chris shrugged out of his tuxedo jacket and draped it around her shoulders, while Jack returned to the water to haul Sam out of the lake.

Moments later, Sam lay back in the grass, taking deep breaths. He sputtered, "Damn you, Jack."

"I just saved your life. You might be grateful." Jack turned to Abby and gathered her into his arms. "Are you okay, Abby?"

Shivering from being wet in the cool night air, Abby pressed her face into his wet coat and nodded.

Sam sat up and surprised them when he pulled his gun out of his wet jacket pocket. "I'm still getting out of here. I'll take your car."

"Put it down. The gun's been under water too long. It won't fire," Jack said.

"Why ask me to put it down if you're so sure? It might still work." Sam aimed at Jack and Abby. Her breath caught in her throat. Then Sam pointed to a nearby tree, and pulled the trigger. The pistol clicked. Nothing happened so he threw the gun at Jack.

Jack caught the weapon with one hand before it hit them. "Sam, you're not going anywhere until the police get here."

Then Jack walked over to Sam and struck Sam's jaw with his fist. "That's for Abby, you bastard. Now, you're going to jail for a long time."

Sam held his cheek. His leg bled from the gun wound. "I never wanted to kill her," he said through gritted teeth. "I needed to get out of here."

Jack took the gun. "Tell that to the police. You held a gun to her head, almost drowned her, and aimed a pistol at us. And you broke into Mr. Farrington's safe and stole the contents."

Sam's hands clenched into fists. "You were ruining my life. And James Farrington helped you."

"How can you blame me? I haven't even taken control of McAlister yet? Whatever is going on with your company has nothing to do with me. All I know is that you made your plans to steal from Mr. Farrington, pretended to leave the estate a few days ago, and then snuck back, and now have your pockets stuffed with valuables from his safe. And I know that gift you sent was just a distraction so you could pull off the robbery. Now take the jacket off," Jack ordered.

Sam stripped off his jacket and began to whine. "And I couldn't even have Abby. I saw you two together when I was out in the woods!"

"So you were at the gazebo?" Abby blurted, her face flaming in spite of being cold.

"Yeah, I happened upon you and Jack in that moment that made me want to kill you…just as you were—"

"Pervert!" Abby blasted.

Sirens sounded in the night air.

"Good, the police are on their way." Jack swung Abby up in his arms. "Let's go back to the house, Abby."

Trent picked up Sam's jacket with the pockets still full

of his grandfather's stolen money. "No wonder he couldn't swim. He's lucky he didn't drown."

Unconcerned about the loot, and thinking only of Abby's safety, Jack carried her to his car.

"You're alive," he said in a raspy voice. "I want you to know that I was scared as hell he was going to kill you."

"I'm very much alive, Jack." She raised her trembling lips to his. When he gently lowered his mouth to hers, she was rewarded with a passionate kiss that sent tingles through every nerve ending. She hugged him and never wanted to let him go.

"I thought I'd lost you—again, Abby. I think I'm going to get gray hair early. You know how much I love you?"

"Jack!" she said, smiling through her tears. "You said it again."

He smiled. "Get used to it. I *do* love you. Now, let's get warmed up."

"I am so cold, Jack."

They left Trent and Chris to deal with the police and the arrest of Sam.

CHAPTER ELEVEN

After Jack and Abby put on dry clothes, they stepped outside the mansion and gave their statements to the police. Then they crossed the lawn with a plan to return to Carly and Miles's party. However, they were just in time to see Monica standing next to a cab. Abby couldn't believe the nerve of her ex-roommate to show up at the house again.

Monica gave Jack and Abby a hateful look. "Well, I see Abby survived. I hope you two will be very happy—*not*."

"We hope the same for you and *Vince*, in return," Abby quipped.

Monica blew out a deep breath. "But, Jack, Vince and I... We never…"

Abby could tell Monica wasn't through lying to Jack, but it was clear he could see through her now, too, because he snorted and shook his head.

"You never quit." Jack crossed his arms over his chest. "It's a good thing you're leaving because the police are nearby. It wouldn't take much for me to call them over and make a report on what you did to my rental car, and how you threatened Abby with a bat. Remember, we have plenty of witnesses—a ballroom full."

Monica's chin jutted out. "You wouldn't."

"Monica, mark my words: If you ever come around Abby or me again, the first thing I'll do is get a restraining order against you."

When he opened the door to the cab, Monica sent Abby a threatening look that sent a chill down to her toes.

Abby tensed, and was very glad Monica lived in another state.

"Maybe next time, Monica," Jack said, "you'll think before you hurt other people with your manipulations. But somehow I doubt that."

Monica's mouth twisted into a bitter line before she complied and slid into the cab. She didn't glance out the window as the cab passed Jack and Abby.

Abby sighed. "Whew! I'm glad she's gone."

Jack put his arm around her. "Let's hope she's gone back to Florida for good this time. Come on." They walked back toward the house.

Mr. James Farrington, his grandson Trent, and a few of Jack's cousins were out on the patio discussing the events of the weekend.

Jack's Uncle James blew out a deep breath. "It's a sad day for me. The police just informed me that Ralph Preston's body was found in his study. They suspect his stepson must have stolen money from him, and that he found out about it, as well as what he was planning to do here. Sam must have drugged him so he could have enough time to get out of the country without Ralph alerting the police. Perhaps knowingly or unknowingly, Sam gave his stepfather just enough drugs to kill Ralph. His mother is distraught and telling the police everything she knows."

Dizziness washed over Abby. "So Sam really did murder someone?"

Mr. Farrington nodded. "But let's don't say anything

until after this weekend ends—for the sake of Carly and Miles."

Abby nodded. "Yeah, we need to salvage the rest of the wedding celebration and make this a happy memorable occasion for them."

The cousins all agreed.

As they headed back to the house, Trent said wryly, "Now, Grandpa, you see why it's doubtful that I'll ever marry. This entire weekend has been one big bad omen. So don't expect a wedding for me." Then Trent grinned widely and teased, "Although please do host all the weddings you want for my cousins here."

Mr. James Farrington's body language revealed his disapproval. "Trent, we'll see about that. I just know one day, you'll meet the right girl, and you'll be eating those words. Soon after, I'll hear the pitter-patter of my great-grandchildren's little feet. And my dear Eliza will look down from heaven and be so happy."

Trent's brow furrowed. "Don't throw Grandma into this."

"You *will* marry someday, Trent," Jack said in agreement with Uncle James. He wrapped his arm firmly around Abby. "When you find the *right* woman."

Alex sighed. "Well, I, for one, agree with Trent. If I'm ever granted my divorce, I'll avoid marriage for the rest of my life."

Chris cocked his head and added his two cents. "More and more I see that women can sometimes be treacherous. Monica was a good example. I'm not sure if I can see myself getting married in the future either."

Jack smiled. "All you guys will eat your words. I should place bets on this and make some money."

Carly stepped out of the French doors from the

ballroom, and everyone hushed to silence, not wanting to ruin her night. "You won't believe what happened. Uncle Peter just got engaged to Mrs. Arlington. I don't know if you met her, but she's the widow of the mega-millionaire Mr. Arlington of Arlington-Dress Enterprises."

Jack's grinned. "Well, I hope it's for love."

Carly shrugged. "But I think he just met her for the first time tonight—and they've both had too much to drink."

"Well, I'm going to give Uncle Peter the benefit of the doubt," Jack said. "He's had it a bit rough lately."

"I suppose you're right," Carly said.

Before they could respond, another couple stepped out of the French doors and onto the patio and headed for a secluded area. Abby noticed it was the guy with the comb-over hair—the one who she'd thought had been stalking her. Tonight, he held the hand of a giggling and smiling woman—Carly's shy cousin Stella.

"Who is that guy, Carly?" Abby whispered.

"That's Miles' cousin Phil. Did he bother you? I hope not. His wife died five years ago. He has a hard time in social situations and is really awkward, so I introduced him to Stella. You know how shy she is. They seem to be hitting it off."

Abby smiled. "Good. I'm so glad. It seems like love is in bloom around here."

Mr. James Farrington, Trent, Alex, and Chris went on inside the mansion.

"Abby are you and Jack coming back inside, too?" Carly asked.

Abby nodded. "But before we go in, I want to thank you for what you were doing this weekend, trying to throw Jack and me together. Surprisingly, it worked. However, I'm sorry if Monica ruined things at your reception." She didn't say a word about the theft, her hostage taking, and Sam killing his own stepfather.

Carly chuckled. "Ruined things? It wouldn't be a family affair if something exciting didn't happen. So other than getting rid of Monica, what else happened tonight? You all took off. You even changed your clothes."

"Nothing much," Jack stated. He linked his arm to Carly's, and took Abby on the other side. "I'm sorry Monica ruined your cake." He effectively changed the conversation and steered them toward the French doors.

"That's okay, Jack," Carly quipped. "As you probably *don't* know, because you are a man, we always make two cakes, one for a backup, and another one to start serving. It's a tradition because you never know what's going to happen at one of our family events, or to one of our cakes. There's been several brawls that have landed in the cakes, so nothing surprises me."

"The part with Monica was my fault," Jack admitted. "I brought her here. I've should have known. What a fool I was."

Carly grinned up at him. "You, my dear cousin, are just a man. You can't be expected to know everything about women like Monica. I'm just happy for you that you'll not live your life with that mistake. Frankly, none of us could stand her. You dodged a bullet, dear cousin." She gave him an impish grin. "Well, I'd better go inside. Coming?"

Jack nodded. "Just give Abby and me a moment."

When Carly had gone into the house, leaving them alone, Jack gathered Abby in his arms and beamed down at her. "We did dodge a bullet, literally. What a night. Are you warm now and happy?"

"Yeah. Very happy and happy to be alive, Jack."

"I can't wait to take you to *our* home."

"I like the sound of that, but *we* don't have one."

"You want to start looking tomorrow? I have a particular property I'd like you to see. Another, smaller, historic house that was in the McAlister family. It comes with thirty acres. Needs lots of renovation, but it has great potential and a stable. I think you'd love it, and we can make it our own. Matter of fact, the only reason I wasn't going to buy it was because I couldn't picture myself there with anyone but you."

Jack took her hand and pulled her to a private part of the patio. Warmth washed over her that he would be hers again—as her husband.

He laid a hand on her breast and squeezed, copping a feel, and sending shivers through her. "I deserved that before we go back inside. So much has happened. It seems like forever since last night when we were together."

Abby chuckled. "Yes, it does." She returned the pleasure and copped a feel right back at him.

Jack groaned and stepped back. "We'd better go inside for a while—for appearances sake—then we can head for *bed*." He smiled and took her hand, pulling her back toward the house. "I'm going to let all my cousins be the ones to complain about marriage. I want us to be husband and wife, as soon as possible."

"Yes, boss. And we'll never let anyone come between us again, right, Jack?"

"Yeah, or work. I'll never let work come between us again either, Abby. I promise to always make time for you. I'll be working hard, but my *workaholic* days are over. I'm going to take time to smell the roses."

"Wait. One more thing. One more kiss before we go inside, Jack?"

"Yeah."

Abby stepped into his embrace. He took her chin in his hand, then lowered his mouth to hers. She circled her arms around his neck.

A thrill of desire and happiness flowed through Abby. When he raised his lips from hers, she said, "Jack, I can't wait for our lives together to begin again. You'll always be my white knight. It looks like I'm getting the fairytale after all."

THE END

ABOUT THE AUTHOR

Debra Andrews has loved reading and making up stories since she was a child so it was only natural that she tried her hand at writing. She writes "Glitzy, Sexy, Romances with a Dangerous Twist," with sexy alpha males and the women who fall in love with them. When she is not writing, she's enjoying her family and pets. She is a member of Romance Writers of America and her local RWA Chapter.

****

MORE ABOUT DEBRA'S BOOKS

Thank you for reading ***WEEKEND WEDDING DECEPTION*** (Dangerous Millionaires Series). I hope you enjoyed the story.

If you would like to help others find this book, leave a review on **Amazon.com**, **Goodreads.com**. Even a line or two makes a difference and is greatly appreciated by an author.

Stay connected and sign up for our newsletter. We will send you information about the next book in the series as soon as it is available, and any important updates:

http://www.debraandrewsauthor.com

OTHER BOOKS AVAILABLE BY DEBRA ANDREWS IN THE DANGEROUS MILLIONAIRES SERIES:

(Books can be read in any order and are stand-alone stories)

WEEKEND WEDDING DECEPTION
DANGEROUS PARADISE
DISGUISED WITH THE MILLIONAIRE
HIS WYOMING LAIR (coming 2016)

Made in United States
Orlando, FL
05 August 2022

20588937R00104